I0730176

FROM GOLD TO GLASS

A Story of True Love Lost,
Grief Carried,
and The Price of Seduction

BLANCA DE LA ROSA

ISBN: 978-1-83556-532-2 Paperback

ISBN: 978-1-83556-533-9 Hardback

ISBN: 978-1-83556-531-5 eBook

Book Design by HMDPUBLISHING

CONTENTS

PART III: THE RECKONING — THE RECLAMATION

PROLOGUE

Some moments don't announce themselves. They arrive quietly—without ceremony, without warning. A glance across a crowded room. A voice that lingers longer than it should. A smile that feels like recognition, though you've never met. It's not logical. It's recognition of the soul. A moment that doesn't ask for understanding—only presence. It's the quiet arrival of destiny. Moments like these don't seek permission. They slip in quietly, rearrange something essential—and, on rare occasions, happen twice in a lifetime. And when they do, they rarely look the same.

David Ortiz didn't believe in second chances. Not after Elena. Not after the silence that followed her absence. He had made peace with solitude—not out of strength, but necessity. He had learned to live with the ache, to fold it into routine. But grief has a way of softening the edges of caution. And loneliness—when dressed in hope—can look a lot like love.

Elena's image still lingered. Her gaze was steady, her smile unposed—the kind of joy that lived in her eyes, not in ornament. She was a woman who knew herself and chose him without hesitation. Their love had been quiet, but it had depth. It lived in small rituals: the way she folded his sweaters, the way she touched his wrist when she wanted his attention. Even their silences spoke fluently. She didn't declare love. She lived it—in gestures, in stillness, in the way she made space for him without asking for anything in return.

And when she died, the world didn't shatter. It hollowed.

Grief didn't arrive with thunder—it settled like dust. David carried it in his spine, in his calendar, in the quiet decision to stop buying fresh flowers for the kitchen table. He didn't speak of her often, but she was everywhere: in the warmth of the house, the softness of his voice, the gold band tucked in the drawer beneath the mantle. Her scent still lingered in the folds of the blanket he never washed.

Loss didn't erase love. It repurposed it—into memory, into quiet rituals, into the space he kept open without knowing why.

He hadn't expected the ache to soften. But it did. Just enough to let someone in.

Not every arrival is destiny. Some are detours dressed in light.

Then came Cassandra.

She was light where Elena had been earth. Dazzling, attentive, full of stories and spark. She laughed easily, touched his arm when she spoke, remembered the names of his colleagues and the wine he preferred. She was different—brighter, bolder. And David, still aching but open, let himself believe.

He hadn't been searching for love. But then Cassandra appeared—bright, reflective, offering what felt like a second chance. And for a time, he believed her. Not because it was love. But because the performance was convincing.

She asked about his dreams. His legacy. His plans for retirement. She said she admired his discipline, his devotion. She made him feel seen again—not as a widower, but as a man still capable of building something new.

She mirrored the absence, not the essence. And he mistook that echo for connection.

PART I

WHEN LOVE WAS GOLDEN

"True love doesn't vanish. It settles into silence and stays."

CHAPTER 1

THE GIRL IN BELL-BOTTOMS

At eighteen, David Ortiz knew two things with certainty: mangoes bruised easily, and girls in hoop earrings and bell-bottoms could bruise your heart just as easily—with nothing more than a glance.

And it was precisely one of those girls—the one in the bell bottoms—who stopped his world on an ordinary Thursday in Manhattan.

Manhattan smelled of hot pavement, spilled beer, and ripe fruit. David built mango pyramids—firm, fragrant, fragile. It was a Thursday, early evening, when the automatic doors whooshed open—and in walked trouble in hip hugger bell bottom jeans. The waistline sat low beneath a cranberry leotard, long sleeved with a scooped neckline. Not provocative—just poised. A quiet statement wrapped in trend. Leotards had leaped from dance studios into street fashion, and Elena's wasn't worn for flash—it hugged her with intent, punctuation to her stride.

She moved like someone accustomed to being seen, but unconcerned with being understood. Her scarf tied hair bounced in rhythm. Hoop earrings caught the light. From behind the mango stand, David felt time slow.

She didn't look at him. Offense one.

"Fifteen," he guessed. Too young. Too Americanized. Not like the girls back home—who walked beside their mothers, not ahead of them. Who spoke softly, eyes lowered when addressed. His sisters wore sandals, not platforms.

Elena's stride was too confident, her earrings too bold, her leotard too exacting. She was too much—too vivid, too unapologetic, too everything he wasn't used to.

And yet, that excess intrigued him. He wasn't sure they'd be compatible—night and day—but something about her unsettled the part of him that believed women should wait to be seen. He didn't dislike it. But it startled him. She moved as if she didn't need permission. Like she'd rewritten the rules others were still trying to learn.

He leaned slightly, offering a smile. "You like mangoes?"

She barely glanced. "I like not being spoken to by strangers in supermarkets."

Offense two.

David laughed, warm and undeterred. "Fair enough. Just the produce guy—consider me invisible."

She rolled her eyes and disappeared into the cereal aisle, her mother chatting in Spanish beside her. He knew better than to follow. She was too everything. But it was her refusal that intrigued him.

She kept appearing—always Thursdays, always beside her mother. He began timing his shifts to her rhythm. Not pursuit—just proximity. Sometimes she glanced. Sometimes not. David began waiting. He shaved closer. Stacked melons cleaner. Rehearsed five syllable openers.

What he didn't know: she was the daughter of the guy from the barbershop who'd once asked him to help repair his Buick. The neighborhood was a net of names and glances. Her mother's hairdresser—his own sister—had mentioned her more than once. Elena had even dropped off her mother's wig for styling.

One afternoon, while chatting with his best friend Luis Delgado—Junior, as everyone called him—and Marisol, Junior's girlfriend, David described the girl who came in on Thursdays. She always wore bell bottoms that swayed with intention, and hoop earrings that caught the light like they belonged to someone older, someone already sure of herself.

"She moves like she's got somewhere better to be," he said. "Like the aisles are too small for her."

Junior laughed, but David wasn't joking. Marisol tilted her head, watching him with quiet amusement. He spoke not like someone nursing a crush, but like someone baffled by awe. He didn't know her name. Just fleeting glimpses. Failed conversations. A handful of moments that made everything else go dim.

Still, the way he spoke—half wonder, half confession—made Marisol smile. She'd seen it before: a boy circling something unnamed.

"I think you're describing my cousin Elena," she said. "She mentioned some annoying guy in the produce section near the mangos. Said he kept staring at her. Kept trying to talk to her."

David froze. Now he had a name. Elena.

The following Thursday, he tried again—this time with ammunition. "Hola, Elena."

She looked startled. "How do you know my name?"

He grinned. "Your cousin Marisol is my best friend's girlfriend."

She blinked. "Good for you. Glad to see you have friends. I'm not one of them. Stop bothering me."

David just smiled. He didn't push. Not yet. He kept to the fruit. Kept to the rhythm. And waited. Because the girl who stormed past him like thunder might just be lightning worth catching.

The following week, during a visit with Junior, David pulled Marisol aside. His voice was low, almost sheepish. The words had been simmering.

"Would you tell Elena something for me?"

Marisol gave him a look. "Why don't you tell her yourself?"

He sighed. "I would—if she gave me the time of day. She won't even look at me."

She tilted her head. "You sure you want to go down that road? She's not exactly sugar and sunshine."

David smiled, soft and steady. "I know. I'm not chasing her. I just think she's worth knowing."

"She's fire, David. She doesn't do small talk. One look, and you're toast."

"I've experienced the look," he said, half in jest, half in hope. "Guess I'll have to speak slowly."

That night, Marisol passed the message casually. "That Dominican guy at the supermarket—the one with the mangoes—he said he'd really like to get to know you. No pressure. Just a conversation. His name's David."

Elena didn't hesitate. "Doesn't he get the hint? Is he slow? I've ignored him every single week. If he thinks I'll ever talk to him, he's more delusional than he looks."

When Marisol repeated the response, David just smiled. "She speaks with conviction. I like that," he said. "It's a start."

Later, alone with the echo of her voice—sharp, unyielding, unforgettable—David stood in the produce aisle where she'd once passed him without pause.

He didn't need her to like him. Not yet. He just needed to stay near the spark long enough to learn its language. Because if she ever let him in, even an inch, he wanted to be ready. Ready to meet fire with grace—and not flinch.

Before Elena—before the Thursdays, the mango pyramids, and the sharp dismissals—there was the long road that brought David to aisle ten in the first place.

Reina Ortiz had been the first to cross that road. At nineteen, she arrived in New York in 1967 with more resolve than belongings, determined not to chase adventure but to build a foundation. Within two years, she had married a quiet man from East Harlem, secured her residency, and petitioned for her parents and siblings to join her. She had come first, but never alone; every step she took was tethered to the family she carried in her heart.

The Ortiz family arrived in 1969 with two suitcases, four dreams, and a silence stitched with sacrifice. They weren't adventurers—they were immigrants, blinking into the metallic, snowy air of JFK, hoping to carve out a better life. Their small Washington Heights apartment held crowded rooms, shared beds, and the kind of gratitude that grows only in families who endure hardship together. Complaints didn't pay the rent, so no one complained. Hardship wasn't failure—it was passage.

They worked long hours. Teresa bagged groceries and learned English through register prompts. Luz washed hair at a salon and handed half her tips to their mother, Carmen, who ironed shirts in the kitchen while humming boleros. Julio walked to the temp agency each morning, hoping for something permanent. Six months later, they had saved enough to move to the Bronx, grateful to return to Reina and her husband the privacy they had sacrificed.

But David stayed behind in Manhattan. He was drawn to the West Side's pulse—merengue on stoops, fried plantains in the air, bookstores filled with Latin American poets and rising Black voices. He had been sixteen when he stepped off the plane—old enough to understand distance, young enough to carry hope without hesitation.

English tangled on his tongue. Hallway slang moved too fast. Teachers spoke too quickly. He learned by watching, absorbing, and translating the world one phrase at a time. He didn't raise his hand; he memorized instead. He survived by listening more than anyone else.

But there was one language that needed no translation: numbers. Math didn't mock. It didn't rush. It didn't demand perfect pronunciation. It waited.

David solved problems in his head faster than others could reach for a pencil. He was a quiet prodigy — precise, steady, constant. Math lifted his grades, steadied his confidence, and years later would lead him to study finance — not out of convenience, but out of clarity.

But numbers didn't fill the silence between classes.

He found his people among other Spanish speaking kids—outsiders like him, bonded by the same ache to belong. They shared translations, stories, heartbreak, and hope. Years later, they would still call each other brother.

By 1973, he had finished high school, enrolled in community college, and worked nights stacking fruit. While others clocked out, he practiced pronunciation, studied market trends, and quietly built a blueprint for his future.

Love, though—love was a different currency. And nothing in his careful plans had prepared him for the girl in bell bottoms.

And now, standing once again in aisle ten, David understood something simple and startling: every step of the journey that had brought him to Manhattan — every cramped apartment, every late-night shift, every English phrase learned by ear, every number solved in silence — had somehow led him here. To this supermarket. To this Thursday. To the girl in bell bottoms who didn't even look at him.

All the years of sacrifice, the long road from Santo Domingo to the Upper West Side, the quiet determination that shaped him — it all converged in the moment she walked past him without a glance.

And something in him, subtle but steady, recognized that this fleeting moment carried a weight he couldn't ignore.

The boy who had crossed an ocean, learned a new world, and rebuilt himself through numbers and silence... stood in aisle ten, watching the girl in bell-bottoms disappear around the corner.

Not defeated. Not discouraged. Just waiting — calm, patient, certain.

Because some storms are worth enduring. And some lightning is worth catching.

CHAPTER 2

RELENTLESS PERSISTENCE

Months passed. David and Elena still hadn't had a real conversation—just one-liners tossed across the produce aisle on Thursdays, like coins into a wishing well. Marisol became the unofficial courier: another message, another plea for her attention. This time, she delivered it with gum snapping and a grin so smug that Elena nearly slammed the bedroom door.

"He said," Marisol smirked, "that if he doesn't marry you, he'll never marry anyone."

Elena rolled her eyes so hard it gave her a headache. "Tell him to get comfortable with bachelorhood. I will never marry him."

They sat cross-legged on Elena's carpet, sifting through cassette tapes and vinyl while their mothers gossiped in the kitchen. Marisol leaned against the dresser, twirling her gum like she was directing a telenovela.

"You sure?" she teased. "He's kind of cute. Got that quiet–mango-seller–turned–mechanic vibe now."

Elena scoffed. "He looks four or five years older, talks like he just got off the boat, and smells like engine grease and mangoes."

She said it like a math problem that refused to solve—David Ortiz: too earnest, too accented, too fresh off the boat.

"He's a time capsule in work boots," she added. "Probably thinks romance means walking behind a woman in case she trips on her own heels."

Marisol cackled.

"I'm just saying," Elena shrugged. "He's too everything. Too polite. Too serious. Probably folds his socks with military precision."

Still, the words felt rehearsed. She pressed play on a bolero—not out of curiosity, but to drown out the possibility that he'd gotten under her skin.

She paused. "And he's always trying to get my attention. Every Thursday—one-liners, weird smiles, loitering by the mangoes like it's romantic. I swear, he's allergic to boundaries."

"You're dramatic," Marisol said, grinning.

"No. I'm strategic," Elena snapped, clicking a lip gloss shut. "You know how many times I've detoured through the bread aisle just to avoid him?"

The memory was immediate: cereal boxes she never meant to buy, fake cramps, volunteering to stand in line while her mother fetched cilantro. But it never worked. Her mother always had a list. And David? Always there among the produce, composing still lifes out of apples and mangoes like it was an art exhibition.

Elena groaned. "You know the worst part? My mom always sends me to ask him something—'Are the mangoes ripe?' 'Do these look fresh?' Every time she says, 'Go ask the produce guy,' I want to sink into the tile."

Marisol tilted her head. "But you still go."

Elena rolled her eyes. "Because I'm a good daughter. Not because I want to talk to the fruit guy. Honestly, sometimes I just wander off and come back with a made-up answer."

Still, she could feel it—that look. Unhurried. Quiet. Unshakable. Like he was waiting for something she hadn't given permission to offer. And she hated that.

Marisol raised an eyebrow. "You really think it wouldn't work? You're both Dominican. You speak the same language."

Elena snorted. "Barely. He speaks English like it's borrowed—careful, deliberate, always reaching for the right word. I live and think in English. It's the language of school, of survival, of sharp comebacks and subway announcements."

She didn't say the rest aloud: He reminded her of everything she'd had to outgrow. Too Dominican—too rooted in old-school manners and Santo Domingo nostalgia. He stood too straight. Smiled too gently. Like someone raised to ask permission before breathing. Elena had grown up in a city that didn't wait for politeness. You moved fast or got left behind.

She'd learned to talk sharp, move quicker, and keep her guard up. He probably thought she was too Americanized. She thought he was stuck in a time capsule. They weren't opposites, exactly—but they were raised on different sides of the bridge.

And then there was the age gap. Not dramatic, but enough to keep their worlds on different tracks. They moved in separate circles, which is why—despite living half a city block apart—they'd never met. Elena's friends were younger, fast-talking, Americanized—girls who lived in English, flirted in slang, and danced to disco remixes. David's crowd was older, quieter, Spanish-speaking men who lingered outside bodegas, played dominoes, and talked about car parts. She didn't see herself in his circle. Didn't want to. It wasn't just the years—it was the rhythm.

The only place their worlds collided was on Thursdays at the supermarket—in the produce section beneath fluorescent lights, where routine masked coincidence and glances lingered longer than they should.

No matter how she zigzagged through the store, he was always there. Polishing apples. Stacking oranges. Arranging basil like it deserved center stage.

Her mother, oblivious, would call: "Elena, get cilantro. No, the fresh kind—smell it first." Or: "Ask the produce guy about the mangoes."

She'd groan, approach like marching into battle—eyes averted, steps deliberate. If he said hello, she nodded. If he smiled, she stared past him like she was searching for papayas that didn't exist.

She didn't like attention—especially the kind that lingered.

Although he was always there, he never pushed. Every Thursday, she found herself scanning the produce section, eyes darting between citrus bins and stacked greens, mapping escape routes before she even picked up a basket. If he was there, she needed a plan—how to pivot, how to vanish, how to limit the time she'd have to face him. But he never took Thursdays off. No matter how much she planned, he was always there, a steady presence she couldn't shake.

And yet, he never pushed. Never followed. But somehow, that made it worse. His restraint had gravity—quiet, constant, impossible to ignore.

CHAPTER 3

DESTINED TO CROSS PATHS

Elena Fernández remembered the smell of linoleum before she remembered the flight from Santo Domingo. She was six when they landed at JFK in 1963—old enough to walk, young enough to feel her mother's grip tighten. The buildings looked like stacked shoeboxes. The air stung her nose. Nothing sounded like home.

Their apartment in Manhattan sat on the fifth floor of a brownstone built for many but made for none. Three bedrooms. One bathroom. A space of necessity, not comfort—walls thin enough to hear arguments above, lullabies below, and televisions to their left and right. Privacy was a luxury. Silence, a negotiation.

They adapted—not just to square footage, but to proximity. Other families lived stacked around them, each carrying their own noise, their own grief, their own version of survival. The Fernández family learned to move carefully, speak softly, and sync to the rhythms of shared living. The building didn't offer solitude, but it offered shelter. And that, for now, was enough.

Her parents—Ramón and Miranda—held the household together with exhaustion. Carla, the eldest, charmed teachers. Jorge, the youngest, broke rules. Elena lived in between—emotionally and literally.

She didn't speak unless asked, didn't laugh unless prompted. Her voice felt foreign—slow, uncertain, dragging two languages that never quite fit. In family photos, she rarely smiled. Not out of defiance, but because something always felt missing.

Her aunt Silvia visited once a month—loud heels, louder advice. "You're too serious," she'd say. "You gotta laugh at this world or it'll eat you alive." Elena nodded but didn't change. She believed the world needed more witnesses than performers.

Books became her refuge. Language, her armor. She copied poems into notebooks, memorized words that tasted like home: soledad, ternura, sombra. Commercial jingles and song lyrics stuck easily. They had rhythm. Structure.

By fourteen, Elena had mastered how to fade into a room while still seeing everyone. She knew how to want quietly.

So when David first looked at her—mango in hand, smile uncertain—she didn't flinch from fear. She flinched because she recognized something. Someone who understood quiet. Who didn't need her noise—just her presence.

Elena was destined to walk into David Ortiz's life—even when she tried not to. Even when she buried herself in routine and reason. Their paths curved relentlessly toward each other, like magnets under glass—pulled close long before either could name the force.

David worked diligently at the supermarket, patiently waiting for Thursdays. Six months of stolen glances and whispered messages—delivered by Marisol, the ever-glittering courier of gossip. He had exchanged only a handful of real sentences with Elena. A few near the fruit stand. No words, just rhythm. Still, she lingered in his mind.

Most days, he considered giving up. He knew when fruit had passed its prime. Maybe hope had, too. She would likely never say yes.

Still, he remembered the first time he saw her—a young teen composed, standing beside her mother in the produce aisle. He might have smiled. Might have lifted a mango like a question. She rolled her eyes and disappeared behind the avocados. He tried to forget. But she stayed.

He meant it when he told Marisol, "If I don't marry her, I'll never marry at all."

So he kept stacking mangoes. Kept watching on Thursdays. Kept wondering why he wanted someone who only said no.

Elena didn't know David was her father's "car guy"—the one who lent tools and talked baseball. Or that her mother's trusted hairdresser was David's sister. They lived half a city block apart. Shared streets. Shared air. Shared the soundtrack of merengue wafting from second-floor windows. And yet, for months, they remained strangers.

Looking back, Elena would say the universe had tried everything—grocery stores, broken-down Toyotas, Dominican beauty salons—not for flirtation, but for recognition. Paths bent, errands rerouted, glances mistimed. Still, they kept finding themselves within reach, like destinies folded into routine.

Fate had already chosen them. No drama. No rain-soaked confessions. Their beginning wouldn't be fireworks—it would be familiarity. A glance held too long. A quiet, nameless feeling. The sense of I know you—before anyone said a word.

Because some lives don't collide. They braid slowly—thread by thread, moment by mundane moment. Until one day, it's clear: they were always heading in the same direction.

CHAPTER 4

THEIR FIRST DANCE

Elena had spent months dodging David Ortiz—his glances, his questions, his quiet persistence. But the universe had already written a different story that was meant to play out.

The shift came at one of those unforgettable apartment blowouts in Manhattan, late summer of '72. Luis, her cousin's boyfriend, was turning nineteen, and everyone from the block showed up. The living room pulsed with shoulder-to-shoulder dancing, bass booming from tower speakers balanced on milk crates. Ice clinked in the bathtub beneath a blanket of beer and soda.

Elena arrived early to help Marisol set up. She'd bought new platform sandals—the kind you don't buy to stay home.

She saw him first, standing in the kitchen doorway in a plain white T shirt, wearing a look usually reserved for poker chips or prayers. I can't seem to shake this guy, she thought. But destiny does what it does.

No wave. No smile. But the moment she stepped in, his posture shifted—shoulders squared, attention locked. For the first hour, they didn't speak. Yet every time the music changed—Aretha to Eddie Palmieri—his eyes found her.

Then her favorite merengue dropped—fast, irresistible, the kind that pulled her in before she could resist. David saw her sitting alone, tapping her feet to the beat, and recognized a window—a chance to approach without words. He stepped forward and extended his hand. No invitation spoken. No answer given. Just a pause. A breath. And then—Elena reached back.

It was the first time she met his gaze without deflection. The first time he reached for her—and she didn't pull away. No way she was missing this. Not even if it meant dancing with David—the last person she'd have chosen. But he was the one who asked, and she was the one who said yes—without saying a word.

Something shifted. Not loudly. Not visibly. But it did. And neither of them could pretend otherwise.

They danced—not intimately, just the steps. Elena moved with crisp rhythm, hips sharp, smile unreadable. David kept pace—not perfect, but confident. He leaned in and asked, "How old are you?"

"Soon to be fifteen," she replied.

He blinked, surprised. She looked sixteen. Maybe seventeen. When the song ended, she stepped away. No eye contact. No words. Just quiet. But as she walked off, rhythm fading, she thought, At least he knows how to dance. Has moves.

Later, while fishing a cold soda from the tub, he stepped beside her.

"You still walking past me like I'm invisible?"

She didn't flinch. "You still using your friends to send middle-school love notes?"

He laughed—slow, unbothered. "Fair enough. Next time, I'll say it to your face."

"I'd still say no."

"Then I'll keep asking."

She walked off with her soda, hips swaying—and smiling.

Weeks passed. David hadn't made real progress with Elena—just a handful of glances, one merengue, and messages passed through Marisol like folded notes in a crowded hallway. Still, he couldn't shake her. So he tried one last move—a soft invitation wrapped in food, family, and the illusion of casual.

Via Marisol, he invited Elena and her sister to a Sunday get-together at his sister's apartment. Not a party. Just music, food, cousins playing dominoes on vinyl-covered tables. Marisol and Luis would be there, and she begged Elena to come, even for a little while.

Elena hadn't planned to go. But Marisol didn't want to show up alone, and Elena had nothing better to do. She agreed, her sister in tow.

David met her at the door—quiet confident, wearing cologne she recognized from the produce aisle. Back when he was just the mango guy.

He smiled, ushered her in, handed her a plate, and introduced everyone—cousins, aunts, even his godfather. His mother sat like a queen at the edge of the room, watching guests as if they were contestants in a talent show.

Then, without warning, David placed a gentle hand on Elena's shoulder.

"Everyone," he said, "this is Elena. My girlfriend."

The room paused—just long enough for the word to land.

Her eyebrows twitched upward, the closest she'd allow herself to a public What.

Her sister choked on tamarind punch.

Marisol shot Junior a look that said, Did you know about this?

Elena didn't confirm. Didn't correct him. Not because she agreed— she absolutely didn't. But she wasn't about to embarrass him. Not with his mother watching. Not with so many eyes softened by joy.

About an hour later, ready to leave, she asked to speak with him privately. He was excited. Maybe even hopeful.

"You ambushed me," she said.

"I said what's true."

She stopped walking. "I'm not your girlfriend. We're barely talking. We've never had a full conversation."

"Then let's start properly." He extended his hand, mock-formal. "My name is David Ortiz. And I have a message for you: I know it sounds crazy, but I feel it—like we're meant to be together. Don't you feel it too? We keep crossing paths like the universe is trying to say something. Elena... why not give destiny a chance?"

He paused, eyes steady. "I meant it when I said—if I don't marry you, I won't marry at all. Because I believe in this. In us. Even if you don't yet."

She blinked, stunned. Scoffed. "You're delusional. Which part of no do you not understand? I meant it when I said you should get used to bachelorhood, David. I will never marry you."

She rolled her eyes so hard the stars nearly rearranged themselves. Then walked away.

He didn't chase her. Just stood there, hands in his pockets, and called softly to the wind between them: "You'll see."

The truth was—she'd noticed. Not just how David watched her like she was a math problem he couldn't solve. But how he never looked at anyone else that way. Not the customers. Not the girls who flirted by the fruit stand. Just her.

Something shifted after that. He had hutzpah. And Elena—freshly fifteen—decided it might be time to give him a chance. Not a declaration. More like a test drive.

A week later, David called to apologize. To his surprise, Elena picked up.

"Elena, I'm sorry. I didn't mean to ambush you."

"I accept your apology," she said. "Let it be the last—because next time, I won't answer."

He paused. "So... does that mean you'll be my girlfriend?"

She traced the edge of a cassette tape with her thumbnail. "It means I'm not hanging up."

For a moment, all he heard was static. Then his smile widened.

"I'll take it."

"Don't," she said quickly. "Don't take anything. I'm not promising you anything."

"Not even a test run?"

"You're lucky I answered the phone."

"Then I'm already ahead of yesterday."

She bit back a smile she didn't want him to hear.

"This doesn't mean yes," she said.

"Got it. But maybe... It's not exactly a no."

She let the silence stretch—like an unopened envelope. The click of her thumbnail against the cassette was the only sound. Then, gently:

"You have one chance, David. Don't make me regret it."

"Never."

In the weeks that followed, Elena didn't admit anything—not to Marisol, not to herself. But she stopped rolling her eyes so hard. She stopped pretending not to hear when her mother asked about mangoes. And when David smiled, she didn't look past him. She looked at him. Just for a second. Long enough to register the quiet steadiness in his gaze. Long enough to wonder if maybe—just maybe—the universe wasn't done folding their paths together. Not yet.

She stopped detouring through the bread aisle. Walked straight to the mangoes. Her mother asked about ripeness. This time, Elena didn't pretend not to hear.

She turned to David. "These look good," she said.

He nodded, surprised but steady. "They're perfect. Almost as perfect as you."

Elena had spent most of her life wondering if mirrors were honest— or just cruel. Raised between two siblings who seemed effortlessly photogenic and a mother whose elegance belonged in magazines, she often felt like a misplaced brushstroke in a perfectly painted family. Her sister Carla wore beauty like a garment. Her brother Jorge had the kind of bone structure that drew compliments in bodegas. Even Miranda, their mother, moved through rooms with a grace Elena never felt she could emulate.

So, Elena became the quiet one. The watcher. The girl whose features never earned praise—not because she lacked worth, but because no one had thought to name it aloud.

Until David.

He wasn't theatrical. He didn't try to impress. He was curious—not just about her voice, but about her silences. One afternoon in Riverside Park, he looked at her with no pretense in his eyes and said simply, "You're beautiful."

She didn't laugh. She didn't blush. She challenged him.

"You only think that because you love me. And we all know love is blind."

His reply was soft. Certain.

"Then may love never learn to see."

That moment stayed. Long after the seasons changed. Long after their hands grew familiar and their laughter took root. It was why she gave him a chance—not because he asked.

CHAPTER 5

A SLOW BLOOM

Their story didn't begin with fireworks. No cinematic kisses. No declarations under moonlight. It started slower—familiarity layered over time, like warmth rising across a sleepless night.

After David's bold declaration at his sister's party, Elena didn't retreat. She didn't rush forward either. She let the moment settle—like steam rising from a cup, unsure whether it would cool or deepen.

She returned to school, clocked in at her part-time job, and tried not to replay his words: *I know it sounds crazy, but I feel it—like we're meant to be together. Don't you feel it too? We keep crossing paths like the universe is trying to tell us something. Elena... why not give destiny a chance?* She couldn't tell if it was ego or prophecy—or both. But it lingered.

David didn't press. He didn't chase. He simply showed up—steadily, gently. A phone call. A walk. A question asked without expectation. His presence became a rhythm, threaded through her days like a quiet melody she hadn't realized she'd memorized.

They began to talk in earnest—not just in one-liners or passing remarks. At first, they spoke in fragments, both testing the boundaries of something beginning to bloom. Then with intention. Walks stretched longer. Laughs lingered. And somewhere between silence and conversation, Elena began to lean in—not because she was convinced, but because she was curious.

He wasn't asking her to believe in forever. He was asking her to believe in possibility.

Her parents noticed first. Her mother, who knew David's sister Luz from the Dominican salon, had always spoken fondly of her—"una muchacha decente, con manos benditas." She remembered the time Luz stayed late to fix a botched dye job for a nervous Quinceañera, refusing payment, saying, "It's her day. Let her shine."

So when David came around, her mother called him *de buena gente* before Elena ever considered it.

Her father saw loyalty in the small gestures—how David lent tools, offered rides, helped with the car, and lingered after dinner to talk baseball. He wasn't flashy. He was steady. Familiar. Safe. And serious.

The night David's mother made arroz con leche, she set an extra spoon beside Elena's—one of those quiet, old-school gestures Elena recognized as a cultural sign of approval, an invitation into the family. That's when Elena said yes.

Later, as they stood at the sink in a kitchen warmed by music and laughter, David handed her a towel and asked—softly, like testing gravity:

"So... are you my girlfriend yet? Or should I ask again tomorrow?"

She dried a plate without looking up. "Depends. Do you plan to stop asking?"

"Not unless you say yes."

She looked at him—the guy behind the mangoes, a man who waited with patience, not performance.

"Then yes," she said. "But only if you promise never to call me *mami*."

He grinned—slow, grateful. "Deal."

They dated for three years—growing between movie nights, house parties, dinners with both families, whispered worries, park strolls, and late-night calls that ended in quiet. Familiarity became foundation. And one morning, without ceremony, David asked the question he'd been carrying for years—nourishing it quietly, trusting that Elena would arrive in her own time.

"Will you marry me—be my wife, my life partner?"

Elena didn't roll her eyes. She didn't hesitate. She kissed him.

Four years had passed since aisle ten—since a girl in bell-bottoms vanished behind the cereal aisle and a produce clerk forgot how to breathe. Now they stood beside each other in her family's apartment, hearts full, hands steady.

When they announced their engagement, everyone nodded like they'd known all along.

Elena's parents were thrilled. They'd known David for years—respectful, hardworking, from a good family. Her father still said, Ese muchacho tiene valores. Her mother agreed. She'd seen the way David looked at Elena—and the way Elena softened when he was near.

Marisol and Luis were among the first to celebrate. Marisol squealed, already mentally arranging bouquets and fixing her eyeliner. Luis grinned and hugged David like he'd won a championship.

The engagement party was held in the same apartment where Elena had once rolled her eyes at romance. Cousins carried folding chairs. Tías filled the kitchen with arroz con pollo and sweet plantains. Boleros floated through the living room, mixing with laughter. The bathtub was filled with ice, chilling sodas, and beer.

David's sister brought pastelitos. Someone taped streamers to the cracked ceiling. Someone else rearranged the saints to make space for cake.

Marisol led a toast. Luis set up the speakers. Elena's younger cousin tried to sneak a sip of rum punch and was caught by her uncle, who winked but didn't snitch.

When David raised his glass—not just to the future, but to the long road that had brought them here—he kept it simple:

"June 28, 1975."

The room erupted.

A summer wedding. A sealed promise. A chapter the universe had been writing all along.

The ceremony on June 28, 1975, unfolded like the final page of a love story—rewritten with grace. Surrounded by family and friends, they stood facing each other, the air thick with years of hope, uncertainties weathered, and inner doubts calmed.

Pastor Ramírez invited the room to settle. His voice—measured, warm, carrying the weight of decades of blessings spoken over couples—rose above the hush.

"Hoy," he said, "no unimos dos vidas que ya han caminado juntas con propósito. Hoy solo lo declaramos ante Dios y ante quienes los aman."

David's gaze never wavered. Elena's, steady and warm, held a promise that made the room hold its breath. They had come far—not just in miles, but in milestones.

This was no fairy tale. It was a lived in love, held together by choice.

The pastor guided them through the ritual, his words anchoring the moment. Then he nodded to Elena.

Her vows came first—gentle but clear. She didn't promise perfection. She promised presence. A love that would not retreat when life grew heavy. A heart that would stay teachable, grateful, awake.

David followed with words he hadn't rehearsed but had carried for years, each syllable carved from the root of who he was. He vowed to be her shelter and her witness, to honor her strength, to choose her even on the days when choosing felt like work.

Pastor Ramírez placed his hands over theirs, blessing the union with a prayer that wrapped the room in stillness. When he finally said, "Los declaro marido y mujer," the words felt less like a declaration and more like a confirmation of something long understood.

And when they kissed, the applause rose like thunder softened by joy.

Their steps down the aisle weren't showy. Just certain. This wasn't the start of a marriage—it was two lives finally side by side.

Each step saying: We made it.

The reception sparkled with warmth and intention. Soft lighting glowed over tables draped in lace and laughter. The music was live. The stories personal.

Marisol danced with Luis in silver heels. Elena's cousins toasted between bites of flan. David's uncles brought their instruments and played until midnight. Aunts wiped tears between verses. Neighbors clapped along to familiar rhythms. Children twirled in circles, their joy uncontained. It wasn't just a wedding—it was a reunion, a celebration of love that had taken its time and arrived exactly when it should.

Elena's parents watched it all with quiet joy. Ramón raised his glass with pride, eyes misting as he whispered, Ese muchacho tiene valores. Miranda, elegant as ever, smiled at David like he was already family—because he was. They didn't just approve. They adored him. Not for grand gestures, but for the way he made Elena laugh, the way he listened, the way he stayed.

David's family welcomed Elena with quiet warmth. They saw what David saw—her sharp tongue, her city polish, her American rhythm— still, they understood. She was a balance to his steadiness, a spark to his calm. His mother once said, Ella es distinta, pero lo hace bien. She didn't try to become someone else. She simply showed up. And over time, they saw how she softened him, how he steadied her. It wasn't a perfect match. It was a true one.

Near the dessert table, tucked between tiers of cake and pastries, sat a simple tray of sliced mangoes—ripe, golden, glistening. David's only request. Not explained. Just placed.

Elena spotted them instantly. She nudged him with a look that said, You sentimental fool.

"You remembered," she whispered.

He leaned in, voice soft. "Every Thursday. Every aisle. Every version of you."

The mangoes were more than fruit. They were history. They were persistence. They were her.

Later that night, beneath a sky scattered with stars, Elena and David stepped outside to catch their breath. The laughter of guests floated behind them like music on the breeze. But out there, it was just them. No spectacle. No performance.

He wrapped his arm around her waist. She rested her head lightly on his shoulder.

"We get to build now," he said.

Their private dance came after the crowd had gone. No announcements. No cameras. Just two hearts moving in perfect time—slow, intentional, a rhythm made for two.

It was the same rhythm that had shifted everything. That merengue in Manhattan. That glance held too long. That moment when silence gave way to movement. Somehow, their souls spoke best through music. It was how they stayed in sync. How they spoke without speaking.

The mangoes remained on the table, untouched but luminous. The night felt endless. Their love, even more.

CHAPTER 6

DANCING ACROSS CONTINENTS

The first six months of Elena and David's marriage unfolded like a quiet dream—brimming with laughter, discovery, and the kind of love that surprised her with its steadiness. It wasn't dramatic. It was daily. And somehow, that made it feel more permanent. But her hand in his, his gaze always seeking hers, made even uncertainty feel like home. They were still getting to know each other, yet the connection already felt timeless.

David was everything Elena had hoped for—gentle, attentive, fully present. He made her feel seen in ways she hadn't realized she needed. In return, she gave him everything: her trust, her heart, and a belief strong enough to hold their future steady.

Their days followed a rhythm of shared wonder—city strolls, spontaneous train rides, rooftop lunches, quiet bookstore wanderings. Evenings belonged to them: candlelit dinners, slow walks through Central Park, whispered conversations that stretched deep into the night.

They were building something deliberate, with love at its center. It wasn't flawless—it was real. And that made it cinematic in its own quiet way. The world fell away, and in the stillness, only each other remained.

Love gave them rhythm. Ambition gave them direction. David had completed his finance degree and was working at a brokerage firm on

Wall Street. Elena, still pursuing her studies in International Business Management at Pace University, juggled lectures, late-night study sessions, and a part-time job at the neighborhood bookstore.

They lived in a modest one-bedroom apartment in Queens—small but softened by comfort. Bookshelves bowed beneath novels and business journals. Secondhand furniture wore mismatched pillows and blankets folded with care. Sunday mornings smelled of café con leche and ripe mangoes. Evenings hummed with merengue, salsa, boleros— and Elena's laughter, low and rich, the kind that made David glance up just to catch her smile.

Their marriage wasn't extravagant, and it certainly wasn't perfect. It was stitched together by loyalty, shared vision, and the kind of intimacy that grows through daily rituals: folded laundry, synchronized calendars, boundaries respected. They didn't blur into each other. They remained distinct—David with his quiet steadiness, Elena with her sharp wit and restless mind.

He was passionate about thoroughbred horses. Saturdays at the track with his friends were sacred—coffee in hand, betting slips folded, eyes trained on the finish line. Elena never asked him to stay home. She knew the rhythm of his joy.

She, in turn, was drawn to legal dramas and true crime. She'd spend Sunday afternoons curled up with a book or lost in courtroom films, dissecting motives and verdicts with Marisol over flan and coffee. David never rolled his eyes. He knew the thrill of her curiosity.

They didn't try to change each other. They didn't compete for space. They gave each other room to grow, to breathe, to be. And then, always, they returned—to mango Thursdays, to shared dinners, to the life they were building together.

It wasn't a fusion. It was a partnership—one where individuality wasn't sacrificed but safeguarded. Like dancers who know when to lead, when to follow, and when to move side by side. Somehow, that made the love deeper. Not louder. Just true.

They weren't perfect. Arguments flickered—about groceries, finances, whether merengue belonged on the Saturday cleaning playlist every week or just every other. But even in tension, they stayed tethered.

When one drifted, the other reeled them back—with a warm meal, a steady gaze, or a hand resting gently on a shoulder.

And always, there was music. A rhythm that belonged only to them. They danced through joy, through silence, through disagreement. It was their unspoken language—the way their souls stayed in sync when words fell short. In kitchens, at weddings, in the middle of living room floors, they moved together like memory and instinct. It wasn't just dancing. It was how they remembered. How they returned to each other.

Elena hadn't married David on impulse. Their decision was grounded—shaped by mutual respect and practical hope.

From the start, they agreed: she would finish her degree before starting a family, so they could fully enjoy each other first. They were young—young enough to believe they had time. Their plan was simple: build enough career stability to support their shared dreams. Travel together, explore new countries, try new restaurants, and live as adventurously as two people in love could. Children would come when the time was right. They wanted to lay a strong foundation first—because kids deserve stability, and that's exactly what they were working toward.

When Elena graduated from Pace University with a bachelor's in international business management, David celebrated as if it were his own triumph. In 1982, she was hired as a financial analyst at Mobil Oil Corporation in midtown Manhattan. David framed her offer letter like sacred text.

That was David's nature—never to outshine, always to uplift. His life revolved around Elena—not from duty, but from a love that was quiet, constant, and instinctive.

A year after Elena began working full-time, they had saved enough for a down payment on a house. They left their Queens apartment behind and bought a modest single-family home in Rockland County—chosen not just for its quiet charm, but for the life they hoped to build inside it. Three bedrooms: a master, and one for each future child they dreamed of welcoming. The backyard stretched wide enough to imagine swing sets and slides, a sandbox tucked beneath shade trees, and laughter echoing across summer afternoons.

The house was wrapped in trees and bordered by a quiet stretch of sidewalk where they sometimes danced without music. The living room glowed with sunlight and carried those same mismatched pillows—soft reminders of the life already unfolding, and the family they longed to fill the rooms.

As their careers blossomed, so did their hunger for more—travel, languages, unfamiliar landscapes. Puerto Rico, where they danced barefoot through a hotel rainstorm. Portugal, two years later—David hopelessly lost, Elena refusing the map just to prove a point. The Dominican Republic again and again, their favorite escape: air like memory, nights like cinnamon and coconut.

They danced everywhere—on balconies, across foreign tile floors, between countertops and record sleeves. Music was their pulse: boleros on Sundays, salsa while cooking, R&B ballads just because. It was their soul language—the way they stayed in sync when words fell short.

Weekends brought slow dinners and boleros, wine glasses sweating beside cookbooks propped open with wooden spoons. In that home, they built routines in rhythm: calendar magnets on the fridge, muddy boots by the door after market strolls, music drifting through freshly painted rooms. Elena hung wind chimes outside the front door. David planted tomatoes in mismatched pots out back. It wasn't flashy—but it was theirs.

As their lives steadied, the dream of something more arrived softly—notes scribbled in margins, sketches tucked into drawers. Elena toyed with baby names in the back of her planner. David imagined how their children might look. It wasn't urgent. Just sweet. A possibility that bloomed quietly between deadlines and folded laundry.

But even music has pauses.

CHAPTER 7

WHEN THE MELODY SHIFTED

It was 1983. They'd been married eight years. She was twenty-six. He was thirty. And they were finally ready to start a family. That's when the first headache arrived—small, persistent, like a note slightly off-key.

At first, Elena brushed them off—long days, stress, too much coffee. She rubbed her temples, downed aspirin, and brewed peppermint tea. "Just a migraine," she said.

David wasn't convinced, but he didn't press. He simply watched. And knowing Elena as well as he did, he noticed the subtle shifts: the way she paused mid-sentence, searching for words she used to summon without effort; the flicker of confusion when she misplaced her keys; the dimming of her usual spark. Dizzy spells came and went. Her balance faltered once in the kitchen, and she laughed it off—but David didn't. Something felt off.

They had time, they told themselves. Before actively preparing for a pregnancy, they agreed to wait—just long enough to rule out anything serious. So instead of obstetrician referrals, they turned their attention to something Elena had quietly envisioned for years: their tenth wedding anniversary, set for June 28, 1985.

Focusing on the anniversary helped quiet the what-ifs. It gave them something joyful to hold on to—something beyond the headaches, the worry, the waiting. And for Elena, it was fun. A distraction, yes, but also a dream she'd been nurturing for years.

To Elena, it wouldn't just be an anniversary. It would be a sacred threshold: ten years of marriage and fourteen since she first met David at a produce stand in a Manhattan supermarket. Those moments stayed with her—a brush of hands over mangoes, casual laughter under humming fluorescents, two lives unknowingly circling the same center. Unassuming. Magical.

But beneath the surface, this celebration was more than tradition. It was Elena's tribute to fate—to the invisible synchronicity that had guided their steps toward each other. The pull of the universe. The quiet gravity of cosmic connection. His persistence. Her resistance. The slow, undeniable momentum that had drawn them together—and held them there still.

She wanted to celebrate the thread. The surrender. The mystery. The choreography of love—steps learned over time, movements shaped by memory. They wouldn't just be marking time. They'd be honoring joy—built through mangoes and music, arguments and reconciliation. A joy chosen again and again.

She began orchestrating the celebration like a symphony—flowers from her favorite shop in Queens, friends invited from Houston, San Juan, and the Dominican Republic. Their first dance would be the same merengue they danced to in 1972. Every detail held meaning: tin for ten, a hope for gold at fifty.

Music existed before the diagnosis—before prayers and hospital rooms. It lived in the corners of their home, spilling from kitchen radios, echoing off balcony tiles, breathing through curtains at dusk. Elena and David moved through life in rhythm, slow dancing over steaming arroz con leche, swaying to boleros in hotel rooms scattered across the globe. They didn't just dance. They lived inside the melody.

Travel and music set their tempo, and they believed—without question—that joy, once nourished, could stretch across decades.

But as their tenth anniversary approached, the music began to change. Soft at first. Then sharp. Elena's headaches returned like a wrong note—minor, then dissonant. She brushed them off, called them migraines, nothing serious. Not enough to skip work or cancel dancing in the living room.

David noticed. He listened the way one does when rhythm shifts. Her steps faltered now and then. Her laughter took longer to rise. She lingered at windows too long. Touched her temple too often.

He asked gently. She smiled gently back. And somewhere in the silence between aspirin and assurances, they both knew: the song was changing.

Their love had always moved in rhythm—steady, deliberate, resilient. But now, the melody was slipping. The harmony thinning.

David didn't push. He never did. But he stayed close—watching, waiting, listening for the notes that no longer landed where they used to. And one evening, after Elena paused mid-sentence and rubbed her temple with a wince she couldn't hide, he reached for her hand and said, simply, "Let's not guess anymore."

She didn't argue. Not this time.

The next morning, she called the doctor.

That call led to a whirlwind of appointments, tests, specialists, and long hours in waiting rooms. And now, they were waiting again. Not for symptoms. Not for guesses. For answers.

CHAPTER 8

PARA DESPUÉS

They were waiting for answers. Not devastation.

August 4, 1983, began with tea and cautious hope—David watching Elena stir her cup a little slower than usual, her smile slightly delayed. The headaches had lingered too long. The tests had multiplied. But neither of them expected catastrophe. Just clarity. Maybe a name for the discomfort. Maybe a plan.

By late afternoon, they sat anxiously in the sterile waiting room of their doctor's office, surrounded by the hum of fluorescent lights and the quiet rustle of paperwork. Days had passed since the tests and scans, and now the weight of uncertainty filled the air, making the silence feel heavier than any noise.

"Elena Fernández," the doctor said gently, breaking the stillness as he read from the chart, his voice softening to cushion the blow, "You have glioblastoma. Stage four."

Silence. David blinked. Elena stared. "What is glioblastoma?" She asked, her voice barely above a whisper.

"It's an aggressive form of brain cancer," the doctor said. "It starts in the brain itself—not from somewhere else. It grows fast, infiltrates healthy tissue, and rarely shows obvious symptoms until it's advanced."

"But I've only had headaches," Elena said.

He nodded. "That's often how it begins. The brain compensates for a long time. By the time we notice cognitive changes, fatigue, or balance issues, the disease has usually progressed."

"What is the prognosis?" she asked.

"Less than a year. With treatment, eight to twelve months."

She looked at him steadily. "And without treatment?"

The doctor hesitated. "Three to six months, on average."

Elena nodded slowly, absorbing the weight of his words. "I'd rather have that time. I want to be present—with my family, with myself. I don't want to spend what's left recovering from surgeries or fighting through chemo. I want clarity, not survival at any cost."

David reached for her hand. This time, she held on.

She turned to him. "We'll dance until the very end, okay?"

He said nothing. But the answer was already there—in the way he held her hand, in the silence that lingered between them. He would keep dancing. Because he wasn't ready to let go of a life that still had moments worth living.

Time didn't stop. It tilted. And David's world tilted with it—off axis, off rhythm, off course. The woman he had built a life with was slipping away, and there was nothing he could do but hold on.

Shock settled between them like fog. Days blurred into one another—time fragmented by restless nights and silent moments heavy with unspoken fears. Elena trembled—not visibly, but in quiet ways: gripping his hand tighter, folding laundry only to pause mid-motion, staring off toward something only she could see.

David offered comfort where he could—soft jokes, her favorite meals, scented candles, music. But none of it reached the place where fear lived. Still, he stayed close.

After the diagnosis, Elena didn't speak much about dying. But her actions began to whisper it.

She started with small things—labels on the backs of photographs, names penned in careful script. Her jewelry box grew sparse. She quietly gifted pieces to nieces, goddaughters, and to Marisol—the one who had kept her connection to David alive in the early days. "They should be worn now," she said gently. David understood what she meant.

She curated memories the way others planned futures—deliberate, reverent, sacred. As if preserving love was its own kind of immortality.

She didn't fear death. Her spirit was rooted in faith—in angels watching, in a life that continues beyond breath, in a universe where love transcends form. She believed that death didn't end a relationship; it simply transformed it into a spiritual one.

What pressed on her heart was the thought of David alone, standing in the stillness of a world where her laughter no longer lived. So she left herself everywhere. Not in grand gestures, but in traces: a playlist's rhythm. A half-used journal. A recipe scribbled in the margins of a Dominican cookbook.

As her body faded, she wove herself into the spaces he would carry forward. If she couldn't walk beside him, she would become the ground beneath his feet. And though she would be gone, she would never go away.

Elena would walk with him always—unseen, unheard, but ever near. Watching over him. In morning coffee. In the soft echo of their favorite songs.

She tucked love notes where time wouldn't find them easily—months, maybe years after she was gone. One tucked into the lining of his winter coat. Another slipped between the pages of his favorite book. Each one signed: Always yours, E.

One morning, while folding laundry, David opened the linen closet and found a sealed manila envelope tucked between the towels. It read: Para después. He didn't open it. Not while her voice still echoed through the hallway. But he pressed it to his heart and stood still for a long time.

In the quiet hours, when the house slept and her body ached, Elena wrote in her journal. Not for the doctors. Not even for David. Just for herself. She kept it tucked in the drawer beside the bed, beneath a stack of postcards from Lisbon and faded ticket stubs wrapped in ribbon. On its pages, she didn't pretend. She told the truth—her deepest thoughts and quietest fears.

There's a quiet that comes after bad news. It doesn't roar—it hums.

Low and constant, behind everything. Even laughter sounds different when it's nearby. I haven't told David how profoundly sad I really feel. He sees glimpses—I know he does. The way my hand trembles reaching for tea. The way I linger at the window too long, staring at nothing. He thinks he's hiding his sadness from me, too. But grief—even in its earliest form—has a scent. It clings before it arrives.

When the doctor said, "Less than a year," I didn't cry. I thought I would. I thought I should. But instead, I looked at David and tried to memorize his face—the twitch of his mouth before he spoke, the way he held my hand like it was anchoring him to this world.

Eight years. We built a life through dancing in kitchens, wandering the world, becoming a 'we' that felt unbreakable.

Now, my body has declared war on itself. I have to find a way to say goodbye to all of it without falling apart.

How do I prepare you to live without me?

You think I'm strong. Brave. But the truth is—I don't want to go. I don't want to leave you alone.

I want one more Sunday morning wrapped in your arms. One more trip we'll never take. One more playful argument over salsa in the living room.

But if I can't have more... then let me have grace.

Let me go knowing I was loved without condition. Let me leave you with music and mangoes and something in your soul that still believes in love.

We'll dance until the end. And after that—I'll find a way to hold your hand.

David took a leave of absence and never looked back. He had made a promise—in sickness and in health—and now, in the darkest stretch of that vow, he was keeping it.

The sound of the heart monitor became constant, a rhythmic reminder of life's fragility. Each beep, every shift in tone, made his own heart race.

Every moment at Elena's side felt like a battle. And still, he clung to hope—that the woman he had loved for so long would fight, too. Days became weeks. David's world narrowed. He was no longer just a husband. He became her caregiver: holding her hands when she couldn't move, speaking for her when she lost her voice, becoming her strength when hers had run dry.

It wasn't easy. It was exhausting. But David never hesitated. Never wavered. He focused on her—on the life they had built together—and the quiet prayer that somehow she wasn't suffering too much.

He fed her. He bathed her. He did what he'd never imagined—and did it with the grace of a man whose love had matured beyond romance, into something sacred.

Family and friends rallied. They called, visited, offered meals, shifts, prayers—anything to lighten the load. The support was abundant, sincere, and constant. But David declined. Not out of pride. Not because he thought he could do it alone. But because Elena wouldn't want anyone else. She trusted him. And in her most vulnerable state, that trust was sacred.

So he remained—no longer just a husband, but her lifeline in the slow fading of light. In that final chapter, David preserved her dignity. One heartbeat. One kindness. One breath at a time.

Elena's decline came quickly. Each day grew slower. Shadows stretched longer. Her body softened and grew still. David stayed close—feeding her, bathing her, managing medications. Whispering stories. Playing songs. Speaking gently, even when words no longer reached her ears.

On the night of January 29, 1984, just after his goodnight kiss, David lay beside her, holding her hand. Her final breath arrived with peace—and left behind a silence no words could fill.

He stayed there, hand in hand, for a long while. Not wanting to let her go. Not ready to make it official. He didn't call family. He didn't notify hospice. Not yet. Not while her warmth lingered in the sheets. Not while her presence still hovered in the room. Tears fell without sound.

And somewhere in the silence, she was still holding his hand.

In the days that followed, David clung to routine—making coffee, folding her sweaters, turning on the radio to their station at the usual hour.

Each act was a memory in motion, a way to keep her close without saying her name.

He tried to preserve something—anything—that still felt like before. But everything had shifted.

The home they built now echoed with absence. Laughter had gone quiet. Light dimmed. And the future—once shared—now stretched ahead: weightless, wide, and heartbreakingly silent.

Still, David would never forget. From the first glance in a Manhattan supermarket produce section to her final breath. From mangoes to music. From thunder to tenderness. From first glance to final breath. It had been his sacred honor to be her caretaker. He wouldn't have wanted it any other way.

His only wish had been simple: to spend every waking moment beside her. And he had.

He would never forget—every dance, every trip, every echo of her laughter—the life they had stitched together through quiet devotion and loud joy. A life now etched into him like a song he'd never stop hearing.

And somewhere—soft as breath, steady as faith—he could still hear her voice: "And after that—I'll find a way to hold your hand."

In the quiet that followed, he believed her—not just as beautiful words or poetry, but as something real, something true.

That night, as David turned off the kitchen light, he let the bolero play a little longer. He didn't dance. Not yet. But he let the rhythm settle into the corners of the house, just as it once had. No longer to summon her.

Now, simply to keep her company.

Outside, the jasmine pressed toward the windows. The garden didn't wait for permission to bloom. And David—grief-worn but not grief-broken— whispered the words out loud: "Te amo, Elena."

Not as a goodbye. But as a continuation.

CHAPTER 9

THE SHAPE OF HER SOUL

The silence was not gentle. It settled like fog—clinging to curtains, folding itself into the spaces between teacups and towels. It wasn't just quiet. It was the echo of her absence, humming through everything she once touched. The air felt heavier than grief.

For the first time since meeting Elena, David moved through life without rhythm. No boleros on Sundays. No dancing in the kitchen. Just silence. Just air. The refrigerator hummed. Wind threaded through the window frames. But none of it registered as sound. Elena was gone. And the world—his world—had lost its music, its purpose. Nothing seemed to matter.

He felt hollow the moment the door closed behind her absence. Days blurred. Nights crawled. Every breath felt borrowed—stolen from the life they used to share. "I'm dying," he whispered once. "Dying just to hold her again."

It wasn't cinematic grief—not collapse or public sobbing. It was quieter. Like erosion. Like being worn down by memory. He was fading in increments. Life drained the color from his dreams. The urge to stretch toward morning, to engage with the living, vanished.

He no longer reached out to the outside world. Current events, family updates, and even the drama of friends held no interest. He cocooned himself in their bedroom, surrounded by her memory—her scent still lingering in the sheets. David's grief was so deep that even breathing felt heavy. Elena had filled every breath with meaning, and now each inhale carried the ache of her absence.

Without Elena, afternoons turned shapeless—like hallways without doors, leading nowhere. He drifted room to room, passing through echoes. Her absence had a sound. It reverberated in cabinets she used to open, drawers she once organized. Nights tasted like sorrow, dense and unforgiving.

He kept conversations short. Abrupt. Not out of anger, but reverence—for the quiet he shared with her memory. He told himself he was fine. Smiled politely. Answered "I'm doing well" when friends reached out. But lies wrapped in courtesy couldn't hide the truth.

She was gone. And in her absence, grief didn't roar. It whispered. It moved through every object, every memory, asking again and again: Who are you now that she's no longer here?

David stood at the threshold—where she used to walk in with groceries, laughter, and plans. He stared longer than he meant to, unsure if he was waiting for her or simply remembering what it felt like when waiting meant something real. He used to know what a day was: shape, purpose, movement.

Now, it was survival. Mornings were harder than nights. Nights brought sleep. Mornings carried expectations—and Elena had infused them with rhythm. Salsa playing low. Coffee brewing. Her footsteps crossing the threshold like punctuation.

In the garden, he sat with folded hands, watching petals tremble. The rose bushes she planted bloomed early. Jasmine clung to the trellis like it still believed in summer. But the scent meant nothing. Her laughter—the thing that used to wake up the garden—was gone.

Passing the mirror, David caught his reflection—like a stranger wearing his face. His eyes had lost their anchor, floating in a face that no longer knew where it belonged. Grief had redrawn him—same outline, different soul. "How do I pretend this is real," he whispered, "when it feels like a bad rehearsal for a life that wasn't meant to unfold?"

He hadn't figured out how to wake up. Because waking up meant letting go. And letting go felt like erasing the shape of her soul.

He woke each morning expecting her voice. Made coffee for two. Poured a second cup. Set it at the table where he imagined she'd sit. At dinner, he still turned up the salsa—hoping to summon her laughter from another room. It never came.

He wasn't mourning a person. He was mourning the shape of her soul—how it had once fit perfectly beside his.

Elena had filled their home with pulse, with presence. And now, even the walls felt hollow.

He folded laundry with robotic care, paused at the linen closet. That's when he saw it again—the envelope.

Para después.

Still there. Still sealed. Still waiting.

He held it in his hands and sat on their bed. He had seen it many times since her death, touched it even, but never opened it. Not because he feared her words, but because reading them would make it real. She had written to a world that didn't include her.

Four months had passed since Elena's death. And today, something shifted. The envelope, once unbearable, now felt inevitable. He could no longer pretend it wasn't time.

Now...

it was *después.*

He traced her handwriting with his thumb on the edge of their bed—the same bed where they had whispered dreams and tangled limbs across seasons. Curved. Deliberate. Still warm with intent.

He opened it slowly, careful with the seal. Inside, a letter folded twice. The paper smelled faintly of lavender.

Her words were waiting:

Mi amor,

If you're reading this, it means I'm somewhere your eyes can't find me. But please know—I'm still with you. In every rhythm you walk to. In every quiet you try to fill.

I hope you danced this morning. I hope the coffee was strong and the sun kind. I hope the world didn't feel too sharp without me. But if it did—that's okay too.

You were never just my husband. You were the keeper of my laughter. My best friend. My confidant. The love of my life. The witness to my becoming.

I lived fully because I loved you freely. You gave me that.

I've left bits of me behind—on playlists, inside books, in drawers you rarely open. Find me slowly. I want you to stumble into memory the way music finds the heart.

And when you're ready, I hope you travel again. I'll be sitting next to you on the plane. Holding your hand. Keeping you company.

You will never be alone.

Walk through cities we loved. Dance in hotel rooms. Live like I'm still twirling beside you.

You'll find my voice in old postcards and mangoes. In the scent of jasmine on summer nights.

I'm not gone. Just quieter.

And maybe... closer than you think.

Siempre tuya, Elena

David folded the letter gently, as if closing a prayer. It lingered on his nightstand—not something he reread every day, but something he often touched—his fingertips tracing the edges, as if reminding his body what love feels like when it's been memorialized.

Eventually, he had it framed. The lavender scent clung to its folds. And each morning, it greeted him—not with words, but with presence.

Thinking of Elena—of their time together—was how David coped. It was his way of keeping her alive, of holding onto the rhythm they had built. Memory became his refuge, his ritual, his quiet resistance to forgetting.

He sat for a long time, letting memory stretch and settle.

Then it came—his first glimpse of Elena. A Manhattan summer. She walked into the supermarket with her mother, long hair tied with a scarf, silver hoop earrings catching the light. No music. No montage. Just a look. The kind that rewrites something in your chest.

He'd asked, "You like mangoes?" She'd replied, "I like not being spoken to by strangers in supermarkets." Blunt. Unapologetic. Her voice rang in him long after she walked away.

It was more than love at first sight. He'd been pulled into her orbit—drawn by something quiet and magnetic. Her presence shifted his center of gravity, as if the world had quietly rearranged itself around her.

In the hush behind the produce stand, David made a silent promise: If she ever gives me the chance, I'll give her everything.

He hadn't just met a girl. He'd met the force that would shape his life.

Now, almost fifteen years later, David sat in the garden, elbows on his knees, watching a petal fall. The air was too still. Too present.

He had been kissed since Elena's passing—touched, held, comforted—but every embrace felt like a poor translation of hers. She was not replaceable. Not even briefly.

He often listened to one of Elena's favorite boleros—En la vida hay amores que nunca pueden olvidarse. In life, there are loves that can never be forgotten. The melody comforted him, echoing through the house like a prayer. It resonated so deeply; it felt less like music and more like truth because she was unforgettable.

What they had was more than love. It was rhythm. Thunder. A breath so potent it rewrote how his lungs expanded. Even now, when strangers welcomed him into conversation, he only ever heard her voice beneath theirs.

Even joy arrived tinged with absence—the laughter over dinner, the Sunday dancing when they burned breakfast on purpose. All of it lived in his marrow.

He had tried—coffee with acquaintances, walks with kind neighbors, flirtation that felt like imitation. But everything led back to her.

It wasn't tragic. Not even painful anymore. It was simply truth: a love that once made you tremble with joy isn't something time can erase, or another love can replace. Not with distance. Not with distraction. Not with anything.

He had always loved music. Loved dancing. But without her, it wasn't the same. The rhythm was broken. The melody muted. He hadn't just lost Elena—he had lost the rhythm of his soul.

She was the pulse beneath his silence.

As he stood again at the doorway, he walked to the radio—the one that still remembered her favorite station. He turned the dial, and somewhere between static and melody, the music returned.

David wasn't just grieving a person. He was grieving a way of life— one so saturated with love that he'd forgotten loneliness had its own rhythm, its own shape.

He sat in the garden often. Small as it was, it was the one Elena insisted they plant. Daisies. Lavender. Mango saplings that refused to root. "They just need patience," she had said. Now, even the petals seemed hesitant.

The silence in the house wasn't just emptiness. It was memory, echoing through cushions and folded blankets. Her shawl still draped over the couch. Her mug sat untouched in the cupboard beside his.

But in that quiet, sometimes he felt it—a warmth on his shoulder, a breath of stillness, a comfort that felt borrowed from her.

Elena had been spiritual. And in her final days, when her voice thinned and words grew sparse, she whispered to him with absolute certainty: *"I'll always be beside you, cariño. Holding your hand... unheard, unseen, but never far."*

He carried those words like prayer beads—small, sacred. And though she was gone, they steadied him—in garden light, in floorboard creaks, in the hush between heartbeats.

Elena's love was gold. And David knew—his grief wasn't just about losing her. It was about the depth of what they had shared, the devotion that had shaped his every breath. When that love was gone, it didn't just leave a void. It rewrote him.

Even in absence, he could still feel her soul—pressed gently against his own, like a rhythm that never stopped.

She had shaped his life. And now, in her absence, she was quietly reshaping the man he was becoming.

CHAPTER 10

THE ANNIVERSARY THAT NEVER CAME

June 28, 1985. The day Elena had once prepared for with joy arrived without her. Ten years since vows whispered into sunlight. Fourteen years since David first saw her—scarf tied, mango in hand, already unforgettable.

It had mattered to her—deeply. Before the illness, she had planned every detail with joy: She called it their sacred threshold—a celebration not just of time, but of love chosen again and again.

Now, the day arrived without her. And David, who had once imagined dancing with her beneath summer stars, could only sit in the quiet and remember what it was meant to be.

He hadn't felt quite right that morning. A light sweat clung to his skin despite the breeze, his breath thinner than usual. His hands were balmy, his chest tight—not sharply, just enough to notice. But he told himself it was the day. The meaning. The memory. Grief had its own weather, and today it was heavy.

Still, he moved with quiet resolve. Set the table. Folded the napkin. Placed her ring in the center. He would mark the day as she would have wanted—deliberately, tenderly. Despite how he felt, he was determined to honor her.

He sat beneath the fig tree, his eyes tracing the table he'd set—simple, intentional. A single plate. A linen napkin folded with care. Elena's wedding ring lay at the center, catching bits of light through the branches overhead. It shimmered like a heartbeat—still pulsing, still hers. Beside it, a double frame: her smiling photo next to the letter she'd written para después—for what came after. The image and the goodbye, side by side.

This was how he chose to mark the day: just him and Elena's spirit. No guests. No music. Just presence. She had promised him once, twice, countless times: "I'll always be by your side—even if you can't see me." And today, David believed her.

He imagined how she might have dressed the table herself—embroidered cloth pulled tight, candles flickering in mismatched holders she'd collected over the years, basil sprigs tucked beside each plate. Her laughter would've echoed as she repositioned chairs to catch the evening breeze. There would've been music too. Something Latin. Something tender. That old bolero she claimed could mend anything broken.

They had never gotten to renew their vows. But today, David lit candles for promises still standing—ten years stitched through trial and joy, simplicity touched with her elegance.

Now, the garden held only stillness. And David, weighted by memory. Grief settled beside him—familiar, quiet. Today, it had shape.

But grief didn't just settle—it surged. His chest felt heavy, breath shallow. Tears came without pause—not dramatic, but constant. Like something inside him had finally given way. The ache wasn't new, but its sharpness was. This day had always mattered to her. And now, it undid him.

Throughout her illness, he wore a mask of false bravado. He didn't have the luxury of breaking down. He had to be her pillar. So he smiled when she needed strength, joked when her voice faltered, and promised that everything would be fine. He convinced her, himself, and everyone else that he was okay.

But after her passing, he gave himself permission to grieve. And grief found quiet places to live—tight behind his ribs, folded in the laundry he still handled with care. Her memory was always present.

Beneath her photo, the calendar she'd kept rested—sun-faded, fragile. On it, June 28, 1985, in looping handwriting: "The day everything changed. Let's renew it someday."

They had dreamed of growing old in this house. Of marking each anniversary with candles and laughter, children chasing shadows through the garden, stories retold beneath fig branches heavy with memory.

David whispered to no one, "You really thought we'd make it to ten... and beyond." His chest tightened. Not sharply. More like something essential beginning to close. Then came the breath he couldn't catch.

His hand moved to his sternum. Pressure. Stillness. A slow, crushing weight. It wasn't just his body giving way—it was the grief he'd been holding for years, finally asking to be seen. The kind that builds over time, then breaks. The basil blurred. Candle flames doubled.

He scraped back the chair. One step. Maybe two. Then, collapse.

His fingers curled around the edge of the tablecloth, clinging to ceremony. Elena's ring pulsed against his palm. Across the yard, napkins fluttered. Fig leaves shifted overhead. The table—carefully set for memory—remained untouched.

It was the flicker that drew Leah.

She'd seen David earlier that afternoon—setting the table beneath the fig tree with quiet care. From her kitchen window, she watched him place a single plate, fold a linen napkin, and light the hurricane lanterns one by one. The glass chimneys flickered softly, casting a warm, wavering glow that seemed to hold memory itself. He moved slowly, reverently. She hadn't interrupted. It felt sacred, like something meant to unfold in solitude.

Now, hours later, she passed by the window again, a grocery bag pressing into her hip, and paused. The sun had long dipped below the ridge. The garden should have gone dark by now. But one light still glowed—low and steady, like a vigil kept by love and remembrance.

Something felt off. David was usually so precise. He would have extinguished the lanterns by now, tidied the table, returned inside.

But the garden remained untouched. The chairs had shifted with the breeze. Napkins lay scattered like fallen petals. And the stillness—it wasn't peaceful. It was weighted.

Leah stepped outside and walked to the side gate that bordered their yards, calling his name. No answer. Through the slats in the fence, she saw him—crumpled beneath the fig tree, fingers curled around the tablecloth, Elena's ring glinting faintly in his palm.

Her breath caught. The gate was locked, as it always was. She hurried across the street to Michael's house, knocking hard. He came quickly, and together they returned. Michael climbed the fence and unlocked the gate from inside. Leah stepped through, her movements careful, reverent.

Rachel arrived moments later, drawn by instinct and concern. From her porch, she'd seen Leah's urgency—the pause, the sudden rush across the street, the flicker of movement in David's garden. Something was wrong.

Leah had already called 911, her voice low but steady as she described what she'd seen through the fence: David collapsed beneath the fig tree, unmoving, the hurricane lantern still glowing softly beside him.

One by one, they entered the garden. They didn't cry. Not yet. The moment demanded stillness, not sorrow. They stood—as if waiting for music to cue, as if honoring a final vow spoken not in words, but through care: the ring, the cloth, the light.

Michael touched Leah's shoulder. "He meant this to be sacred," he murmured. Rachel knelt beside him, brushing away a leaf. "He made it holy."

No one spoke of grief directly. Not yet. They let the silence mark what words could not. They saw the calendar, the inscription. They saw how memory had been laid out like communion.

And in the stillness beneath the fig tree, they bore witness—not to a man's final breath, but to a love so complete it outlived the body that once held it. She had promised to stay beside him. And she had. Their love didn't end with her death—it simply crossed into the spiritual realm.

CHAPTER 11

THE SLOW COLLAPSE

The stillness beneath the fig tree gave way to urgency—sirens cutting through the quiet, shattering what had moments before felt sacred.

The ambulance arrived within minutes. EMTs found him on the ground, vitals slipping. His own wedding band—removed, pressed into his palm. Beneath his curled fingers, Elena's ring glinted softly, as if ritual itself might hold him together.

At the hospital machines blinked their impartial rhythms. Blood tests confirmed he was in the midst of a heart attack. An electrocardiogram traced the erratic rhythm of his heart. A chest X-ray followed, then an echocardiogram—each test narrowing the possibilities, searching for the source.

His mother arrived first, her hands trembling as she reached for his. Reina, his oldest sister, followed close behind—steady, composed, but visibly shaken. They sat in silence, watching the monitor, willing proximity to steady its pulse.

"He never let it out," Reina whispered. "He joked. He hosted. Even at the memorial—he was taking care of us."

A nurse nodded. "It's common in caregivers. They don't fracture loudly. They erode."

Marisol came next, then Julio, and the others. One by one, they filled the room with quiet presence.

Luz placed a double frame beside the bed—Elena's unposed smile on one side, her para después letter on the other. The same image David had laid beneath the fig branches. Her eyes, steady. Her presence, undimmed.

As the hours and days passed, David stabilized. Quietly. Monitors settled. Oxygen softened the struggle in his breathing. David stirred. His fingers moved. He opened his eyes and saw them—friends and family, gathered around him.

On the third day of his hospitalization, the doctor returned with the results, standing near David's bedside where his family gathered quietly.

"There's no blockage," he said, meeting David's eyes. "Your heart is strong. But the left ventricle shows signs of stunning—likely triggered by a surge of stress hormones. Cortisol. Adrenaline. It's called Broken Heart Syndrome, or Takotsubo cardiomyopathy. A physical response to emotional trauma."

He paused, then continued more gently. "You carried it too long. The body remembers what the mouth doesn't speak."

The doctor turned to the others, his voice low and steady. "Grief isn't always loud. Sometimes it threads itself through ritual, settles into muscle, and waits—until the heart finally asks for rest. This episode wasn't sudden. It was a reckoning. Slow. Accumulated."

David looked up, steady. "Do you think this was the final swell of everything unspoken? The day of her diagnosis. The months of caretaking. The quiet panic. The mask of courage. Her death. And the year and a half of mourning that followed like a shadow?"

The doctor nodded. "Yes. Takotsubo cardiomyopathy is the official diagnosis."

In hindsight, David saw the progression. The erosion had been quiet, gradual—never sudden but always accumulating. The heartache arrived in fragments: her toothbrush still in the cup, untouched. The scent of lavender no longer clinging to the hallway. One less chair pulled up to the table. No footsteps in the morning. No humming in the kitchen. These were the quiet markers of her absence. The daily reminders that she was gone

He smiled for photos. He walked with ghosts. His body bore it quietly, making space where grief settled like sediment. And when his chest finally tightened, it wasn't sudden—it was overdue. The collapse wasn't loud. It was earned. A final ritual of release, shaped by years of quiet devotion.

For David, it was the quiet consequence of remembering without release—the body's rebellion after a year and a half of holding grief in the marrow. A collapse that marked not just pain, but a threshold.

After the collapse—after his body finally surrendered to the weight of everything unspoken—something began to shift. Not healing. Not forgetting. Just space—where sorrow could breathe without breaking him. He still missed her. Fiercely. Daily. But the sorrow no longer clawed at the edges. It didn't unravel him. Grief sat beside him now— quieter. Familiar.

The hardest part had passed. What remained was grief, yes—but not as raw. More lived-in. Not a wound, but a quiet companion.

This wasn't healing in the way people imagine—not a clean break or sudden lightness. But it was a turning point. A loosening. A soft release. The beginning of letting go—not of her, but of the hurt.

In the weeks that followed, David began to move again—slowly, deliberately. Later, he traveled—not far at first, and never in haste. He took slow walks in the park, passing the bench where Elena used to sip café con leche and critique strangers' fashion with loving sass. David smiled quietly, hearing her voice in memory.

He returned to the farmer's market, bought mangoes he didn't need, and watched the vendors cradle fruit the way Elena used to. *"Like it's fragile. Like it matters."*

He visited familiar places—Philadelphia. Old San Juan. Lisbon, again. On the first flight, the middle seat beside him sat empty. But David knew: Elena was there. He wept quietly, remembering their wanderings, her joy, the ease with which she became part of every place. Each city held an echo—a balcony they danced on, a dish she ordered twice (once for taste, once for ritual), a bookstore where she lost track of time.

He moved through each place slowly, letting grief and grace walk together inside his chest.

And sometimes—when no one was watching—he danced. Alone. In hotel rooms. Barefoot in his living room, eyes closed, imagining Elena twirling beside him. It wasn't choreographed. It wasn't joyful. But it was movement. And it belonged to him.

The music returned in fragments—a vinyl left spinning, a radio humming during dinner. One night, while dusting bookshelves, he found her old cassette: *limpieza + música con alma*. He played it, dancing with a feather duster the way she used to. When the song ended, he sat and wept.

He wasn't healed. He was changed. And with each quiet step, he made room—for the ache, for the memory, for the becoming.

He spent more time with friends and family, let conversations linger, let weekends stretch without loneliness as their shadow. He welcomed connection—gentle, unhurried. Kind people. Warm moments. But no one could ever replace Elena.

Not one touch, not one smile, ever recreated the voltage of the produce section. That spark he felt when he first saw her. He shared stories, held hands, listened. But each night, in the quiet, he knew: Elena had marked his rhythm in ways no one could rewrite.

Until one day, change arrived with a new tempo. Quiet at first—like a song playing softly in the background.

David's story, for now, had found its stillness. Not resolution—grief rarely offers that. But rhythm. A life reshaped by memory, reclaimed through motion, held together by quiet dignity.

He had learned to walk beside absence. To live without flinching. To honor what was, without chasing what might have been.

But stories don't end with silence. They echo.

And five years after Elena's passing, on a Thursday with no significance, at a company event celebrating Hispanic Heritage Month, Cassandra Jiménez entered David's life—with a voice he hadn't yet learned to recognize, and a tempo that would quietly alter his rhythm.

Not a replacement—Elena was irreplaceable. A harmony, suggesting that love can grow again. Not by erasing the past, but by echoing it.

David's story didn't end with grief. It continued—with rhythm, with silence, and eventually, with Cassandra. But to understand what came next, we must first understand Cassandra Jimenez.

THE LONG CON
THE ARCHITECTURE
OF BETRAYAL

"He mistook glass for gold."

CHAPTER 12

THE CURRENCY OF CHARM

Cassandra Jiménez had a gift. With just a few well-placed words, she drew men into her orbit and made them believe. No theatrics—just timing, tone, and a glance held half a second longer than expected.

Women, however, were rarely fooled. Where men saw charm, women sensed orchestration—too polished, too effortless. Cassandra possessed that elusive quality that made her unforgettable, but not always trustworthy. She knew how to occupy a room: where to stand, how long to hold a gaze, when to smile just enough to suggest sincerity. Men leaned in. Women kept their distance. Cassandra noticed. She preferred it that way.

Raised modestly outside Newark, New Jersey, she learned early that beauty opened doors—but she didn't just walk through them. She dismantled the locks behind her.

Her lessons weren't taught—they were earned. Cassandra didn't inherit wisdom; she assembled it piece by piece: trading attention for insight, silence for safety, charm for small allowances. She studied survival in kitchens heavy with cigarette smoke and pawn shops steeped in the scent of broken promises. Her mother juggled jobs, men, and overdue bills with the weary grace of someone who'd stopped expecting more. Her father? Gone before she was old enough to memorize his features.

By eight, Cassandra listened more than she spoke. She watched her mother flirt with landlords for extensions, older cousins lie with a smile to get discounts, and how prayers worked less often than polished half-truths. Soft power, she learned, could unlock hard doors.

At thirteen, Cassandra overheard a stockbroker laughing with his friend, gesturing toward her mother. "You don't pay for reality," he said. "You pay for the fantasy."

Her mother didn't flinch. She took a drag from her cigarette and replied, "Men want illusions. Give 'em a good one, and they'll pay for the privilege."

That moment stayed with Cassandra—not as shame, but as instruction.

Fantasy wasn't deception. It was demand. A transaction. A service.

Men weren't seeking truth. They were seeking escape. And Cassandra learned early: if you could become what they were looking for, you weren't lying. You were delivering. She never saw disgrace in that. She saw leverage.

At sixteen, she stepped into a pawn shop in Elizabeth, New Jersey, gold bracelet in hand—the kind passed between her mother's boyfriends like liquor and blame. The clerk was unimpressed.

"This ain't solid," he said. She smiled. "It's real. Just old. Like your cash register."

Two twenties later, she walked out with lunch money—and something deeper. Confirmation. Charm was currency. Intuition could be weaponized. And men? Most were waiting to be studied, sculpted, and spent.

Even as a teenager, Cassandra embraced a brutal truth: rich people had money. Poor people didn't. Smart girls didn't ask for help—they asked for bank routing numbers. Her early cons were small: credit card skimming, fake returns, fast cash. But those were warm-ups. Cassandra wasn't chasing scraps. She was designing the score that would reshape her life.

She graduated high school at seventeen—a year early, with a 4.0 GPA and a portfolio of recommendation letters that read like endorsements. Rutgers Southern had offered her a full ride: tuition, housing, even a stipend for books and travel. Merit grants, leadership scholarships, early admission. They saw promise. She saw a trap.

"I don't need more lectures," she told her mother. "I need leverage."

She packed a duffle, promised New York was only for the summer, and never looked back.

New York City in the early '80s was a city of contradictions—gritty, glamorous, and unapologetically alive. Wall Street was on the rise, the subways were tagged and unpredictable, and Times Square remained more vice than vision. Studio 54 had shuttered, but its afterglow lingered in downtown lofts and rooftop lounges. The city rewarded reinvention—and Cassandra arrived ready to disappear into it.

She was seventeen—street-smart, observant, and already fluent in the art of adaptation. She'd left behind a scholarship and a mother who taught her that illusion was currency. New York wasn't a dream to her. It was a system. And systems could be learned.

She started small: a shared room in Queens, cash jobs, late-night shifts at diners. She studied everything—how tips were earned, how attention was managed, how power moved through a room. By eighteen, she was working coat check at a midtown lounge. By nineteen, bartending in the East Village, slipping into conversations with brokers, DJs, and men who mistook her silence for mystery.

By twenty, she was fluent in the nightlife economy. Cassandra moved like smoke—slipping between rooftop lounges, underground parties, and backdoor modeling gigs. A hostess on Tuesdays. A bottle girl on Fridays. Amused by Sunday brunch and the people who mistook confidence for noise.

Beneath the lashes and lip gloss, she was always watching—tracking eye contact, reading power dynamics, measuring silence and timing. She understood charisma not as charm, but as geometry: angles, pressure, precision.

She had a method.

On weekends, she worked a sports bar in tight jeans, flirting with traveling businessmen. She watched other girls flash new lives through chat rooms—stories of flown-out trips to Miami, whispered upgrades to penthouses and private jets. Cassandra wasn't chasing luxury. She was engineering it.

Every move was calculated. She saved for months—not for comfort, but for optics. Every dollar was an investment in perception: luxury decoys, pro-level makeup, grainy Polaroids that implied a life already lived. She borrowed outfits, attended mixers with her finance-savvy roommate, and curated her presence with precision.

In Cassandra's world, image wasn't accessory—it was currency. First impressions weren't casual. They were leverage. So she smiled like she belonged and let the illusion do the rest.

Her image wasn't autobiography. It was bait. A master manipulator in high heels, she weaponized elegance—turning allure into strategy. She didn't scramble. She orchestrated. Survival wasn't reactive—it was rehearsed. And while most girls were still finding their footing, Cassandra was already building the blueprint.

No broke boys. No small players. She could smell real money in five minutes—fake Rolexes, leased cars, inflated net worths. She went on twenty-one dates in six months. Some harmless. Some creepy. A few con artists themselves. None scared her. She had studied the market.

In that world, seduction was the highest-performing asset. Her magnetism wasn't accidental—it was curated. Controlled.

By twenty-two, Cassandra had mastered the art of social presence: the right blazer at the right brunch, borrowed confidence at networking mixers, and just enough mystery to feel expensive. She carried herself like someone who mattered—without ever having to explain why.

When she walked into a ballroom, she looked like she belonged. Someone important. Someone desired. That was her gift: blending in with moneyed confidence, slipping into circles without leaving ripples.

In 1986, at the age of twenty-three, Cassandra met Juan Diaz at a rooftop event downtown—an invitation-only mixer suspended between skyline and secrecy. He was twenty-five, already seasoned in the New York con game, with the kind of polish that came from years of calculated charm and quiet exits.

Juan spoke with intention, wore cufflinks to casual dinners, and drove cars like he lived—fast, flashy, and never in one place for long. He didn't talk much. But when he did, people leaned in.

Cassandra noticed. She recognized something in him—an appetite for risk, a taste for performance, a hunger that mirrored her own. They were alike. Not in style, but in instinct.

And that made him dangerous—not because he could fool her, but because he didn't need to. They were both chasing the thrill of the con, both drawn to the edge where control and chaos blur.

They began seeing each other in secret. No public dates. Just late-night calls, expensive takeout, and quiet conversations about legacy, opportunity, and the kind of people who'd never see them coming.

By twenty-four, she was in a full-fledged relationship with Juan. Real in feeling. Quiet in exposure. There were no promises. No plans. Only a tacit alliance between two architects of artifice.

They both knew that love could be useful, that intimacy could be leverage. But they also knew that true power was whispered between accomplices who understood the value of a well-timed entrance and an exit without a trace.

Juan studied her. And she did the same.

It was about strategy. About recognizing in the other a possibility.

And in that recognition, Cassandra found something she had never sought: a mirror without judgment. A reflection without correction.

It wasn't love. But it was alliance. And for Cassandra, that was enough.

CHAPTER 13

PRECISION IN THE SHADOWS

Juan hadn't inherited influence. He built it—like a vault: slow, strategic, brick by brick, in the dark, without blueprint or light.

Raised on the east side of Baltimore by a grandmother who believed in discipline, dignity, and discernment, Juan lived by her three unshakable rules:

Never owe more than you can repay. Debt wasn't just financial—it was spiritual. A man who overpromises underdelivers. Reputation, she said, was a credit score. Guard it like currency.

Keep your shoes clean. People look down before they look up. Scuffed shoes meant you'd stopped caring. Polished shoes said you showed up with intention.

Speak only when your words are worth more than your silence. Real power doesn't shout—it waits. Juan learned to listen longer than most, to read rooms before entering, and to speak only when precision was required.

These weren't just rules. They were framework. Beneath every silence, every calculation, they held him together.

He didn't build power by accident. He built it by code—his grandmother's code. And in every deal, every room, every negotiation, her voice echoed beneath his restraint.

Shoes polished. Debts counted. Words measured.

Before Cassandra, there were others. Juan was always the architect—never the bait. He worked with dancers, hostesses, even a former pageant runner-up. The faces changed, but the formula didn't. Clean entry. Quiet exit. No mess.

He didn't seduce. He calibrated. While others chased chaos or thrill, Juan chased silence. He studied shame, mapped vulnerability, and built operations on discretion. His partners played their roles—flirtation, fantasy, emotional camouflage—while Juan handled the logistics: bank transfers, secure lines, exit strategies.

He wasn't sentimental. He was surgical. The con wasn't romance—it was a playbook. And Cassandra—sharp, observant, fluent in social geometry—wasn't the first to run it. But she was the first to understand it. Not just the blueprint, but the silence it was built to protect.

To Cassandra, he was proof that power could be quiet. That real architects of ascent didn't announce themselves. They studied. They waited. And when the moment came, they moved.

Together, they ran cons in four states—corporate retreats, tech mixers, charity galas. Nothing violent. Just precision. Cassandra lured. Juan cleaned. Their marks rarely called the police. Shame was a silencer. Most preferred to write it off—an expensive heartbreak.

Married men feared fallout. They didn't want their families knowing where they'd been—or what they'd wanted. Others worried about reputation: the kind of damage that doesn't bruise the skin but breaks careers.

Cassandra and Juan didn't chase chaos. They engineered silence. Their victims weren't typical. They were men who wanted their shame to disappear.

The first was a 58-year-old oil executive in Houston, Texas. Divorced. Lonely. Desperate to feel young again. Cassandra dated him for eight months. He paid for her apartment, her car, and her credit cards. When she vanished with $50,000, he was too embarrassed to report it.

The second was a 62-year-old developer in Mobile, Alabama. Widowed. Depressed. Throwing money at anyone who'd listen.

Cassandra played the sweet, understanding girl-next-door. She walked away with $75,000 siphoned from his savings account.

And there were others. A venture capitalist in Denver. A surgeon in Miami. A lobbyist in D.C. Each one drawn in by Cassandra's poise, undone by Juan's precision. The method never changed—only the names, the cities, the currency. The con didn't end. It simply moved on. One mark after another. One silence traded for another. And in every ballroom, every brunch, every whispered promise, Cassandra and Juan remained invisible—until they weren't.

After three years of profitable vanishings, Juan leaned across the kitchen counter. "We need the big score," he said. "We're wasting your talent on small-time marks. We should think bigger." "Like what?" she asked. "One rich old man. One big score. He sets us up for life."

He framed it as strategy, but underneath was something colder. "Beauty fades," he said. "Men want youth. They want something to show off—hang on their arm like a trophy. It's ego. You've got the look now—why waste it?"

Cassandra poured wine and waited.

"No more boutique damage," he said. "We're done with stylish scraps. We build the long con now—no fast cash. Legacy money."

It started with a blueprint. A model. A future scripted in quiet theft.

"He's mid-fifties," Juan said. "Private equity. Widowed. Still wears the ring—but not the grief."

Cassandra raised an eyebrow. "You've got someone in mind?"

"Not yet. But you'll find him. We're not chasing a name. We're chasing the pattern."

She didn't ask how he knew what she could pull. She just let the design unfold.

"He'll be lonely. Well-dressed. Good teeth. Sentimental. Not flashy. Generous in conversation, guarded on paper."

"Someone looking for softness," Cassandra murmured, "but willing to pay for precision."

"Exactly. He wants redemption wrapped in silk. You'll be the woman who makes him believe again."

She folded her arms. "You want me to make him fall."

"No," Juan corrected. "I want you to make him believe. That he was right to wait. That you are the reward for all his restraint."

She didn't blink. "Then what?"

"Then you marry him."

No humor. No hesitation. Just schematic.

"And after the vows?"

"You extract. Elegantly. Joint account. Tax leverage. A honeymoon that doubles as asset transfer. He won't bring up a prenup—not after you cry, tell him how your mother was left with nothing. He'll think protecting you makes him noble."

"Let him fund the fantasy," she said softly.

Juan nodded. "That's your job. You're the architect. Build the illusion. Let him move in."

This wasn't fast cash. It was legacy theft. Retirement accounts. Investment portfolios. Real estate. Anything with long-term yield. They'd be in and out in under two years—methodical, quiet, clean.

The con wasn't about urgency. It was about access. That was the birth of the long con. Not petty theft—financial reengineering.

The plan was sequential: Step one—find the mark. Step two—charm him. Step three—make him fall in love. Step four—marry him quickly, before clarity could interrupt infatuation.

She didn't steal. Not yet. She studied. She hunted.

Cassandra spent weeks preparing for each networking event. She researched every major donor, memorized their interests, their charities, their scars. She rehearsed conversation starters until they tasted natural.

She chose the perfect dress—elegant but not loud, expensive but not obviously so.

They began scouting for the prototype: wealthy, older, lonely. Cassandra would marry him, gain access to his accounts, and strip them clean.

She let the silence hang, tasting its implications. Cassandra wasn't new to seduction. But this wasn't flirtation—it was civic-level engineering. Identity fraud dressed in champagne and monograms.

"You'll know him when you see him," Juan said. "They always carry the same scent—regret lacquered with ambition."

"And you?"

"I stay invisible. You orchestrate. I organize. We extract. We exit."

Cassandra turned to the window, scanning the city like a résumé. Somewhere out there was her next role. Her next mark. She would find the prototype. And by the time he realized what he'd signed up for, the paperwork would already be filed.

Juan leaned in. "If we're doing this," he said, "we need to be clear. I protect you. You protect me. No witnesses. No liabilities."

Cassandra nodded. Her stomach turned—not with fear, but with clarity. This wasn't a proposal. It was a contract.

Juan reached for her hand. Not affection. Finality. The handshake before the heist—the moment strategy became reality.

That night, the plan began. Not fast cash. Legacy theft.

"Fast money doesn't last," Juan said. "Legacy money can set us up for life."

CHAPTER 14

THE JACKPOT

She hadn't expected much from the gala. Just another ballroom. Another swirl of saxophone and practiced smiles. She didn't attend events. She dissected them.

She was there as a favor to a friend who didn't want to attend alone. Cassandra agreed to accompany her, posing as a real estate agent with polished ease—her name stitched into a guest pass like it belonged to a life she'd never lived.

Cassandra Jiménez was a professional—not the kind who filed reports in glass offices, but the kind who studied wealthy, vulnerable men with quiet, psychological precision. She was stunning: flawless skin, a bright smile, curves that caught the eye and held it. But her true weapon wasn't beauty—it was fluency in desire.

She had a gift for becoming exactly what her mark needed: curious but not naïve, driven but not intimidating. She'd been doing this for years. Wealthy men. Lonely men. The kind who mistook fascination for trust. The kind who wanted someone who "just got them."

And she did. She spoke their language—finance, art, policy, legacy. She could quote Rothko and reference derivatives in the same breath. Her intellect was quiet, precise, and disarming. But it wasn't just book-smart brilliance. Cassandra had street sense—an instinct for power, a fluency in human weakness. She knew how to mirror the cadence of Ivy League boardrooms and the charm of corner cafes. She could read a balance sheet and a body language cue with equal clarity.

She didn't take shortcuts. She created narratives—entire identities tailored for access. Her academic discipline, once aimed at scholarship and escape, had evolved into something sharper: a toolkit for deception. She mastered complex financial schemes the way others mastered piano—methodically, invisibly, with grace.

The plan with Juan—always humming low like a backstage cue— wasn't meant to activate tonight. She wasn't scouting. Just observing. Sipping overpriced champagne and testing the edges of elegance.

But then David Ortiz appeared.

It was September 1989, a Hispanic Heritage Month gala hosted by his company. Beneath low lighting and perfume-laced saxophone, David stood in quiet relief against the noise. Not polished—centered. His tailored suit fit perfectly, worn with intention, not vanity. Widowed. No children. And yet he moved like someone who had long since made peace with sorrow. A man who carried loss not like a wound, but like a pressed collar—present, dignified, softened by time.

David Ortiz was a humble man from humble beginnings—an immigrant with more grit than guidance, who arrived in the city at sixteen with soft hands and quiet ambition. He didn't come with wealth or connections, just a willingness to work and a mind wired for discipline. Over time, he built a future most would envy. But he never flaunted it. No designer suits for impression. No luxury cars idling outside crowded restaurants. Success hadn't inflated him; it had clarified him.

What made David extraordinary wasn't his wealth. It was his heart.

Each December, he quietly donated thousands to ensure children across New York City had gifts beneath their trees, pencils in their backpacks, and books beside their beds. He never wanted to forget where he came from. His journey—from immigrant teenager to self-made success—was stitched with struggle, and he carried that memory like a compass. Giving back wasn't charity. It was continuity.

David didn't just believe in love. He believed in legacy.

As someone who had once felt invisible in classrooms and break rooms, he spent years mentoring young Latinos—the future leaders he swore the world would no longer overlook. It wasn't just his mission. It had been Elena's too. Together, they built that legacy: late nights drafting speeches, weekends hosting college prep workshops, quiet pride as each student walked across a stage holding a scholarship award.

Their work with the Hispanic Heritage Foundation wasn't philanthropy. It was gratitude—a way to honor the community that helped them rise. Every summit, every panel, every scholarship was a mirror: reflecting David's struggle, Elena's belief in him, and the future they had dreamed into being.

He believed that if you could help a child access education, you could place a future within reach. Education was the passport—out of poverty, out of invisibility, into possibility. His focus was always on those who had less: immigrant children, working-class families, kids who needed more than help—they needed hope.

He believed in goodness. In redemption. In family.

He lived in a peaceful home in Rockland County, cradled by quiet woods and birdsong. In the mornings, windows gathered the sound like scripture. The air smelled of pine and folded time. It was serene. Ordered. A space that matched the man.

But despite everything—the wealth, the quiet, the legacy—one note was missing from the symphony: love.

And that night, the melody shifted.

David knew these rooms. Velvet tuxedos. Soft jazz. Business cards flicked like confetti. Polished. Predictable. Forgettable.

Then, across the crowd, he saw her. Cassandra Jiménez. Twenty-six. Poised. Intelligent. Magnetic in a way that made silence feel deliberate.

Their eyes met almost at once. His gaze was steady. Hers, calculating—but curious. In a ballroom full of posture and performance, theirs was a quiet alignment. Not dramatic. Not prolonged. But charged with something unscripted.

Stillness was his signal.

Cassandra noticed instantly. Not because he chased attention. Because he didn't. There was gravity in his silence. Clean lines in his gentleness. A soft dignity that held her gaze longer than she meant to offer.

She adjusted instinctively—not toward flirtation, but toward calibration. The eye contact. The half-sincere smile. The tilt of her glass, timed to the lull in conversation. The performance lived in her bones. But this time, she let the moment breathe.

David was the blueprint. The con required vulnerability wrapped in strength, grief softened by hope, a man who still believed in connection. And he fit the design—too well, too deeply, too easily.

He approached, drink in hand, posture relaxed but deliberate. Up close, he didn't smell of bravado or cologne—just pressed linen and something quietly unplaceable, like memory half-awake.

He hadn't expected anything tonight. Not connection. Not interest. Certainly not that quiet pang—the one he hadn't felt since Elena. It wasn't comparison. It was memory. But when Cassandra smiled, something opened. A door, long closed but never locked.

"Welcome," he said warmly, his voice tinged with a Dominican accent and rhythm that softened every word. "David Ortiz—hosting tonight on behalf of the foundation. Are you with one of our partner groups?"

She smiled, measured and magnetic. "Cassandra Jiménez. Real estate. I'm tagging along with a friend from the finance world. She promised good music and better champagne."

He chuckled, noting the poise in her deflection. "Then I hope we're delivering on both."

"Your suit helps," she said, eyes glinting.

He raised his glass. "Rum, if you're feeling festive."

She accepted, watching the ice shift like a compass. "Festive sounds right."

Their exchange lasted only minutes. A few lines. A glance that lingered one breath past etiquette. Then applause rippled through the crowd as David's name was announced. He offered a parting smile, walking toward the stage with quiet ease.

But mid-stride, before reaching the mic, he turned. Just once. And looked back.

Cassandra didn't wave. Didn't wink. But her smile lingered one beat too long. Like a light left on in an empty room.

It wasn't flirtation. Not exactly. It was recognition. Not of David. Not yet. But of silence that carried something worth chasing.

After his speech, she walked up to him.

"I admire what you do," she said. "It's rare to find someone who shows up so completely—for a cause, and for others."

David smiled. For the first time in a long time, he felt seen.

"It's not easy," he replied. "But it's worth it. That's what keeps me going—I want to make a difference."

Cassandra glanced over David's shoulder. Her friend—the one who'd invited her—was gesturing discreetly from across the room, tapping her watch with a raised brow. Cassandra offered a soft laugh, half-apology, half-exit.

"I promised her we'd leave before the speeches," she said. "Early morning tomorrow."

She thanked him, said goodnight, and offered a polite "nice meeting you." No hint of connection. No promise of more. Just enough to leave the door ajar.

David watched her walk away, the crowd folding around her like mist. He didn't call out. Didn't ask for her number. It wasn't the time-stopping certainty he'd felt with Elena.

But it was something. A flicker. A possibility. And he let it walk out the door.

He told himself it wasn't the moment. That if it mattered, fate would find a way. Still, as her silhouette dissolved into the velvet blur of the ballroom, he wondered—quietly, achingly—if rarity always arrived like this: unannounced, unclaimed, and already gone.

That night, the impression of him lingered—quiet, deliberate, impossible to ignore.

Back home, Cassandra began her research. The gala brochure lay beside her laptop, its linen finish faintly scented with cologne and ambition—proof that wealth always dressed itself well. As the saxophone notes faded in memory, she followed the trail: corporate sponsors, leadership bios, donor lists. Breadcrumbs.

She traced David's name through public records, newspaper clippings, and business filings at the local library. It was a portrait assembled the old-fashioned way: real estate holdings in county registries, life insurance mentions in finance newsletters, society page profiles confirming the absence of children.

Thirty-six. Salsa and merengue dancer. Widower. No children. Net worth close to three million. Every asset in his name—clean, untethered, intact.

David was visible in all the right places. Measured. Composed. Shaped by solitude. Easy to read. Easier to reach.

And Cassandra had learned to read stillness like terrain.

He was the mark.

She folded the gala brochure slowly, creasing it into sharp, symmetrical lines—an origami bloom. A quiet metaphor: elegance restructured for utility. Beauty repurposed for deception.

Then she called Juan. "I met him," she said flatly. "The widower. Hispanic Heritage gala. He hosted it. Thirty-six years old. No dependents. Liquid and fixed assets, all traceable. No offshore distractions. The man's a vault—unlocked."

Juan exhaled. "You think he'll bite?"

"He won't bite," Cassandra replied. "He'll lean in."

The first target had been a miscalculation. Preston Lyle looked ideal on paper—polished, eager, just wounded enough to mimic depth. But Cassandra quickly saw he wasn't grieving. He was performing. His vulnerability was decorative, not penetrable. No fracture. No leverage. Just Scotch, stories, and surface-level charm.

She let him fade—no drama, no damage. A blueprint, not a breakthrough. A rehearsal, not a risk.

David Ortiz was different. Juan called him the big score. Cassandra called him dangerous.

He was wealth wrapped in ritual, grace woven into every gesture, presence shaped by memory. A man who moved with intention—tipped with precisely folded cash, left handwritten notes for waitstaff. Solitary, yes—but far from hollow.

His silence wasn't empty—it was saturated. It shaped space rather than filled it.

She studied him carefully. Tuesdays at Café Luna. Charity events. The way he adjusted his cufflinks mid-conversation, as if it were a gesture passed down from someone he'd loved. He didn't flaunt his wealth—he honored it. He didn't seek attention—he offered presence.

And this time, she didn't just spot the mark. She saw the architecture of the long con.

CHAPTER 15

THE STAGED ENCOUNTER

A month after the gala, Cassandra staged their next encounter—Tuesday morning, just before nine. She'd spent weeks assembling his profile the old-fashioned way: public records, quiet breadcrumbs, and the kind of research that left no trace but revealed everything.

The night before, she studied the rhythm of foot traffic inside his office building—who arrived when, which elevators stalled, and how long the security line delayed movement. She timed her approach with surgical precision.

It wasn't her first attempt.

Two weeks earlier, she lingered outside Café Luna, hoping for a casual overlap. But David arrived late, took his coffee to go, and left without glancing up. She'd worn a silk blouse that day—too polished, too deliberate. Wrong tempo.

Another time, she positioned herself near the entrance of a charity board meeting he was rumored to attend. He never showed. She spent forty minutes pretending to scroll her phone, rehearsing lines she never got to deliver. The timing was off. The rhythm hadn't aligned.

This time, she adjusted everything. She wore a camel wrap dress—professional, flattering, forgettable. Designed not to impress, but to blend in. Hair pulled back. Minimal jewelry. A look curated for coincidence.

She didn't need him to notice her. She needed him to believe he'd discovered her.

Her makeup was soft, her borrowed leather briefcase understated. She positioned herself near the corridor that led from the elevator bank to the lobby, pretending to scan the directory as she walked slowly toward the reception desk.

As David stepped out of the elevator and walked into the lobby, she pivoted—just enough to cross his path.

"Oh—sorry about that," she said, voice bright with apology. "Got caught in the current."

David steadied her with a gentle touch. "No harm done," he said, voice warm but slightly breathless.

Cassandra met his gaze, her voice steady. "Morning rush hour maneuvers—I'm clearly off-step."

He smiled, more than intrigued—almost relieved. "I remember you from the gala. The real estate agent?"

"That's me. Cassandra." She tilted her head, letting recognition land softly. "David, right?"

He nodded, eyes lingering. He'd regretted not getting her number when they first met but had told himself that if it was meant to be, fate would intervene. And here she was—like a second chance dressed in camel and quiet timing.

This time, he didn't plan to let her vanish.

"Would you like to grab coffee?" he asked. "There's a café two blocks over that's decent."

"Sure," she said with a soft laugh. "Caffeine sounds perfect."

They walked side by side. Talked for nearly an hour at the café. Cassandra listened—attentively, without interrogation. She made him feel interesting, not inspected.

He mentioned that he was a widower. He spoke about his work, his routine, Elena, and the weight of loss. She offered just enough truth to maintain the delicate balance of the illusion.

Before parting, he reached into his wallet and handed her a business card—linen stock, embossed name, no title. Just David. She accepted it with a gracious nod. Then, after a brief pause, she took his pen and wrote her number on the back.

No rush. No performance. Just a quiet exchange beneath soft café lights: his card, her number, and a moment suspended between sincerity and design.

"Maybe again sometime," he said.

She smiled. "I'd like that."

When she left, she carried more than a good impression. She carried coordinates. A route. A rhythm. A plan.

Three days later, David called. No suggestion. No small talk. Just a reservation confirmation—delivered like a verdict.

Tavern on the Green.

Cassandra stared at the name. It had shimmered at the edges of conversation for years—murmured in lounges, clipped from society columns, conjured in scenes of romance and excess. Most New Yorkers knew it. Few could afford it. To her, it had always belonged to other people's stories. Untouched. Unattainable. Almost mythical.

She had never been to Tavern on the Green, though its reputation had long lived in the margins of her world. But it wasn't the location that impressed her—it was the precision of the gesture.

A man didn't choose Tavern on the Green unless he wanted the evening to live in memory. And he didn't extend that kind of invitation unless he wanted it to matter.

Cassandra understood that kind of gesture. She respected it.

She arrived early. Heart steady. Heels clicking with quiet resolve against mosaic tile. The garden glowed—hedges clipped, lanterns lit like stage cues. Inside, a tuxedoed maître d' guided her past velvet booths and crystal chandeliers, toward a table positioned with intention: close enough to the jazz trio to feel luxurious, far enough to invite conversation.

The menu offered no prices. Just promised a great meal: filet mignon with truffled foie gras, butter-poached lobster, saffron risotto, and a caviar service so opulent it came with ritual.

David gestured toward the pages. "Order whatever you want."

She met his gaze with a smile calibrated to charm, noting how the chandeliers threw soft halos against the booth fabric, how the wine glasses looked too delicate to grip without intention.

"You don't strike me as someone who skimps."

"I don't believe in half-measures," he replied, voice smooth, eyes steady.

She ordered the lobster dish. He chose the filet. They shared a bottle of Bordeaux with a name she didn't recognize—but a finish she wouldn't forget.

By the time dessert was cleared, she understood. This wasn't about cuisine. It wasn't about spectacle. It was about what the setting whispered—intimacy offered without interrogation, desire folded inside discretion. The invitation was a signal. A man who chose Tavern on the Green was writing a kind of emotional contract: subtle, serious, deliberate. Cassandra read the terms fluently.

She hadn't just gotten through the door. She'd been ushered in— like a guest of honor in a story she hadn't written but now controlled.

Every detail—the velvet, the wine, the way he leaned in to listen— was part of the yield. David was opening himself to believing. And for Cassandra, belief was currency. This wasn't seduction. It was the jackpot beginning to pay out.

David still carried a quiet ache, reaching for something steady to hold on to. Some men move slowly through loss. They seek constancy. Cassandra understood that. So she became what he needed: patient, supportive, empathetic.

She admired his values, mirrored his unspoken pain, echoed his causes. She let him speak about Elena without interruption or flinching. It was performance—finely tuned, like dining with silence between courses.

Cassandra leaned in with practiced gentleness, handling him the way one handles fine stemware: fragile, precious, easy to crack. David watched her—not just for her smile, but for the quiet between gestures.

Something stirred—not desire, not yet, but recognition. He recognized Elena's grace: the way she hummed boleros while peeling mangoes, the way she listened as if every word mattered.

Was it chemistry? Perhaps. Or the illusion of it.

David felt connection.

Cassandra felt access.

To her, romance was a pitch. Intimacy, a transaction. David wasn't someone to love. He was a ladder to prosperity. There was a ten-year age gap. Cassandra didn't mind. It was leverage.

Outside the polished persona, she lived a separate truth. A boyfriend—young, impulsive, real. Secret phone calls. Motel rendezvous. Laughter in places David would never enter.

He accepted the mask. And Cassandra wore it well. Polished. Precise. Designed to ease his burdens and sell an illusion. Every smile, every nod, every pause—calibrated. Not authentic. But convincing.

The signs were there: guarded calls, careful deflections, smiles that stopped just short of genuine. But David, swept up in the promise of possibility, saw only perfection. He had once known true love. And this—this wasn't the same. But it rhymed. And sometimes, rhyme is enough.

By spring of 1990, they were inseparable. During their courtship, Cassandra became everything David needed her to be. She listened to stories of his humble beginnings, asked thoughtful questions, and nodded reverently when he spoke about Elena—how her absence had left him unmoored.

"You're an amazing woman," David told her one evening as they sat on his back patio, watching the sunset. "I can't believe someone like you would want to be with someone like me."

Cassandra took his hand and replied, "Don't say that. You're an incredible man, David. You've built something extraordinary from nothing. I'm the lucky one."

A flawless performance. And David believed every word.

What he didn't see were the moments when Cassandra thought he wasn't looking—the way her expression vanished the instant he turned away, how she rolled her eyes when he mentioned his late wife or his family, how every gesture was rehearsed, every pause intentional.

She was constantly calculating. Planning. Adjusting.

He didn't see that Cassandra wasn't reaching back—not yet. That her warmth, though convincing, was more choreography than connection. The intimacy he began to feel wasn't mutual—it was curated.

What lived behind her gaze wasn't emotion—it was strategy. Measured. Intentional. Already at work.

CHAPTER 16

SOMETHING OFF CENTER

Elena had been gone for five years. Yet her spirit remained—woven into the heartbeats of both families, present in memory, in ritual, in the quiet ways people still missed her. She had been an integral thread in their lives, and even now, she lingered in the textures of the afternoon—folded into laughter that faded too soon, threaded through boleros drifting across the backyard.

Smoke curled from the grill, mingling with citrus and caramelized plantains. Folding tables bowed under arroz con pollo, pastelitos, and memory. A small group clustered near the shed, slapping dominoes in a rhythm older than any recipe.

Inside, David sliced limes slowly, humming one of Elena's old tunes. The barbecue wasn't just tradition—it was continuity. She had once anchored him. Now, in the quiet repetition of slicing and song, he felt her presence—not as ache, but as echo.

This wasn't just a cookout. It was an unveiling.

David had chosen this day to introduce Cassandra to the people who mattered most—to the ghosts still living in every corner of the yard.

She arrived thirty minutes late in a crimson dress with gold accents, heels tapping in time with her smile. She breezed in like someone rehearsing warmth.

David lit up, weaving past chairs and cousins mid-conversation. "There she is," he said, proud. "Everyone—this is Cassandra."

He guided her forward like unveiling a future already imagined. "She's brilliant, beautiful, and patient enough to put up with me," he added.

Cassandra laughed lightly. "And wise enough to recognize a good investment," she said, letting the word linger—half joke, half-truth.

Polite smiles followed—some warm, some slow to settle. A few women exchanged glances, uncertain whether to laugh or bristle.

As David stood beside Cassandra, beaming with pride, his body language said what words hadn't: I want her to be part of this.

He knew his sisters well enough to recognize the pause—the polite restraint that settled just beneath their smiles. So he leaned in, guiding Cassandra forward with a smile that asked for more than approval. It asked for acceptance.

Not everyone received her charm the same way. Especially not Marisol Rivera.

Near the grill, Marisol sliced plantains with precision, her jewelry understated but deliberate. She watched Cassandra—not with jealousy, but instinct. Something about her cadence felt curated. Her warmth didn't radiate—it reflected.

"So, Cassandra," Marisol said lightly, "David said you met at that heritage event in New York."

"Yes," Cassandra smiled. "Hispanic Heritage Month. I was there representing my real estate team."

"Selling condos to culture lovers?"

"Not quite. Mostly client-facing work. But I've always had a soft spot for architecture—especially homes with history. That's what drew me to real estate." She glanced around. "And I've always admired homes like this. David's taste is... refined."

Junior looked up. Luz paused her stirring.

"Refined?" Marisol echoed.

"Yes," Cassandra replied, "the kind of place that says you've made it."

The words hovered—chosen, not felt. Cassandra hadn't been there for work, but the lie was clean, practiced.

"Elena didn't need places to say anything," Marisol said. "She made space speak."

A breeze shifted the tablecloth. Cassandra smoothed the corner—too poised, too aware.

Later, in the kitchen, David dried glasses while Marisol stacked trays. Cassandra's voice floated in from the living room—smooth, bright, just loud enough to be heard. She was telling a story about a client in Miami, something about a penthouse and a broken chandelier. Her laughter was effortless—the kind that filled space without asking permission.

"You're quiet," David said, handing Marisol a glass.

Marisol didn't look up. "Just listening."

David nodded, watching steam rise from the sink. "She's good at that," he said. "Making people lean in."

Marisol placed a tray on the counter. "She's good at performance."

David glanced toward the doorway. Cassandra's silhouette moved with elegance—gestures timed, smile calibrated.

"She's not like Elena," Marisol added softly.

David paused, then spoke—low, steady. "No, she's not. And it's not fair to compare them." He dried slower now, more deliberate. "She may not be like Elena... but I love her."

Marisol didn't respond. She placed another tray on the counter, her movements precise. The word hung in the air—unanswered, unchallenged, but not unnoticed.

Cassandra entered the kitchen, sunglasses in hand, and kissed David's cheek. "Your arroz con pollo was picture perfect," she said, flashing a smile toward Marisol.

Marisol didn't look up. "Perfect's for catalogs," she said.

"We cook with memory—what's passed down, what's felt. What's left after the stories are gone."

Cassandra laughed lightly, undeterred. "I love your people. Such energy."

Marisol paused, then met her eyes. "It's not energy. It's history. The rhythm of old songs and shared grief. Camaraderie. Affection. We don't perform—we remember."

Cassandra's smile held, but something behind it flickered. She registered the weight of Marisol's words—the pride, the warning, the quiet refusal to be charmed.

Her instinct was to pivot, to smooth the moment with warmth and polish. But this wasn't a room that responded to polish. It responded to presence. And presence, she realized, couldn't be rehearsed.

She offered her goodbyes—graceful, practiced, effortless. David walked her to her car.

As the door shut behind them, Luz folded a towel. "It wasn't the words," she said. "It was how she held them." "Like someone choosing lines from a script," Marisol murmured.

Outside, Cassandra buckled her seatbelt and glanced back toward the house. She'd seen the tight smiles, heard the off-notes. She knew she wasn't trusted. Not yet. Maybe not ever. But it didn't matter.

She looked at David, still waving with boyish affection. What mattered was him. What he saw. What he chose. And he had chosen her.

The cookout had been Cassandra's first real introduction to the family. Most had met her then—some for the first time, others in passing weeks before. She had smiled, listened, charmed. But something had felt off. Not loud. Not wrong. Just... rehearsed.

The warnings began quietly. A question from Reina. A pause from Junior. A glance from Marisol.

When David was getting serious—bringing Cassandra to family gatherings, speaking about her with quiet pride—the unease sharpened.

Three weeks later, concern had crystallized into something more deliberate.

The intervention took place in David's living room. Julio, Carmen, Junior, Reina, and Marisol sat in a loose circle. No accusations. Just truth.

"David," Reina began gently, "don't you think this is moving too fast?"

She didn't push. But what could she say? That Cassandra looked at the house like she was pricing it. That she didn't trust anyone that perfect. That the precision felt theatrical.

"She's charming," Reina said. "But something feels hollow. Like she's reading from a script."

"We've seen you at your best," she added. "This version feels like you're trying not to see something."

"There's warmth," Marisol said, "but it's rehearsed. It doesn't match the rhythm here."

"She looks at you like you're something to perform on," Carmen added, "not someone to build with."

"She keeps it surface-level," Reina said. "All shine, no depth."

"She talks about appearances," Marisol added. "Not the everyday stuff that actually makes a life work."

"It's all for show," Junior said. "She sees the house, not the home."

"When she stepped into this house," Reina said, "the awe wasn't about you. It was the view."

"Before asking how you slept," Carmen added, "she asked about the countertops."

"She wasn't drawn to the history," Marisol said. "She was dazzled by the finish."

"Maybe she's looking for more than companionship," she continued. "Security. Stability. A life she hasn't built."

"She sees you as a provider," Carmen said. "Not a partner."

"You're generous," Junior said. "But generosity without caution is a risk."

Silence settled. No ultimatums. Just the request to pause. To wait. To see her without the haze of hope.

Then his father spoke—quiet, measured. "You've known her less than a year, mijo. That's not enough time to know someone fully. Give it another year. Let the seasons pass. Let the quiet moments speak."

His mother nodded. "Love doesn't rush. It reveals. If it's real, it'll still be there."

They had felt the edges from the beginning. Couldn't name them, but they lingered.

David had listened—quietly, respectfully. Defensive, yes. But not dismissive.

He stood slowly, voice steady. "All Cassandra has shown me is loyalty, love, and real interest in me—not just what I do, but who I am. And while I respect your concern, what you're offering is instinct. Gut feelings. Conjecture. None of it is proof."

"I'm going off what I've seen with my own eyes. What my heart feels. These are the same feelings I had for Elena. Was I wrong about her?"

He looked around the room. "No. I wasn't. I see in Cassandra what I saw in Elena—that grace, that steadiness. Even if it's flashier."

"I know she's not Elena," he said. "But she sees me. And after everything... I need to be seen. Above all, I love her."

Marisol met his gaze. "You deserve to be seen, David. Just not distorted."

Junior leaned in. "Different isn't the problem. It's what she does when she thinks you're not looking."

David nodded slowly. The room was quiet.

"I hear you," he said. "I'll keep my eyes open."

One month after the doubts were voiced—softly, urgently, lovingly—the wedding invitations were printed. Her name shimmered in gilded script: Cassandra Jiménez.

To most, she was elegant, magnetic—and unfamiliar.

David was a widower. After five years alone, he finally asked himself: Is it too late to be loved again?

She was twenty-six. No job. No children. No home of her own. But Cassandra had a smile. She had charm. And she said all the things a lonely man hopes someone will still say—even after life has taken so much.

Some called it love. Others called it desperation. For David, longing became a blindfold.

Within two years, it would cost him everything: his savings, his trust, his quiet belief that love—if it came—would come gently.

He had heard the warnings. Seen the hesitation in his friends' eyes. Felt the caution in his parents' voices. But he chose to believe in possibility—in the idea that love could arrive differently. Flashier. Faster. But still, real.

He told himself that happiness, once offered, shouldn't be postponed.

CHAPTER 17

EYES WIDE SHUT

In May 1989, eight months after they met, Cassandra and David married in what looked like a picture-perfect union. The ceremony unfolded in the garden of a small, elegant hotel in Manhattan—intimate, polished, meticulously arranged. Beauty surrounded them. But not everything felt beautiful.

For David, it was love: steady, sincere, rooted in emotional recognition. For Cassandra, it was leverage. His respected role in the Latino community, quiet loyalty, and reliable income gave her the access she needed—not to prestige, but to assets.

To her, the marriage wasn't a milestone. It was a mechanism—strategic, calculated, transactional. A doorway, not a destination.

Reina watched the proceedings with quiet concern. Her brother was a grown man, preparing for one of the most important events of his life, and she wanted the day to be perfect. But something kept her on edge. It wasn't the logistics—not the flowers, the music, or the guests. It was the calculation she saw behind Cassandra's practiced smile.

She had tried to warn David before. His reply had been sharp: "You're overthinking things." Now, on the day of the ceremony, she made one final attempt.

David stood near the archway, adjusting his cufflinks, radiant with anticipation.

Reina approached, her voice low and steady. "David, there's something I need to say before the ceremony. I know this isn't the ideal moment, and we've touched on it before. But as your older sister, I'd be remiss not to speak up."

He sighed. "Come on, Reina—not your gut feelings again."

"I'm not trying to stop you," she said. "I just want you to pause and really think about what you're stepping into. I know you want this to be the start of something beautiful. I know you're tired of being alone. But love isn't just about being chosen—it's about knowing who you're choosing. And the truth is, you barely know her."

He cut in, smiling. "I know enough to know she's perfect. Our relationship is perfect."

"It's not about perfection," Reina replied gently. "It's about how little you actually know about Cassandra."

David turned, his smile faltering.

"She knows a lot about you," Reina continued. "She knows what you value, what you've lost, who you lean on. But you—David, you don't know her. Not really. Not where she comes from."

She leaned in, voice unwavering. "Have you met anyone besides that one brother? Have you been to her family home? Do you know what her childhood looked like—who raised her, what shaped her?"

"She's met your entire family. She's sat at our table, heard our stories, and seen the photo of Elena on the wall. But where's your seat at her table? Where's your glimpse into her world?"

Reina paused. "You're building a future with someone whose past you barely know."

David's expression hardened. "Don't start. Not today."

"I'm not trying to ruin anything," Reina said. "I'm trying to protect you. Because once the vows are spoken, it's not just a celebration—it's a contract. And if she's not here for the right reasons, you'll be the one paying the price."

David exhaled, the tension in his jaw barely softening. "I know you're worried. You always are. You've always been overprotective. But I'm a grown man. I know what I'm doing."

He looked past her, toward the gathering guests, the music beginning to swell. "I get it—the whole family's concerned. But I'm not naïve. I've weighed the risks. I've made my decision, and I'm entering this marriage with eyes wide open. I need you to trust that I know what I'm doing."

Reina studied his face, searching for something—hesitation, doubt, a crack in the certainty. But all she saw was resolve.

She nodded slowly. "Then I hope you're right," she said. "But if you're not, I'll be here to help pick up the pieces. And I know the whole family will stand with you—no matter what."

She didn't wait for a response. Just turned, composed, and walked back toward the crowd, carrying the weight of everything unsaid.

She had always been protective of her younger brother. Not controlling. Not possessive. Just attuned to the quiet things—tone, timing, truth. And today, her gut told her something was deeply off.

The ceremony began in the early afternoon. The sun illuminated the garden with bright rays. Snow-white arches were covered in flowers. Guests dressed in their finest attire watched the couple's every move with smiles that didn't always reach their eyes.

Cassandra wore a sleeveless off-white satin dress—minimal, timeless. Diamond earrings—hers, not borrowed. A cathedral-length veil that kissed the floor. No bouquet. Only intention.

She walked toward David with confidence and ease, her arm lightly looped through Juan's—introduced to everyone as her brother, the only family she claimed. As if the bustle of the festivities were her natural environment.

David, waiting at the altar, looked enraptured. He wore the biggest smile anyone had seen on him since Elena's death. His gaze—full of joy and delight—was fixed on his bride. He couldn't look away from her, this beautiful creature who would now be his wife.

In the front row, Reina sat beside her parents—composed, unreadable. David's mother sat with hands folded, eyes steady, her silence a kind of prayer. Behind them, siblings, friends, and extended family watched with quiet reverence. They had voiced their concerns. They had asked him to wait. But today wasn't about doubt. It was about showing up.

When David and Cassandra exchanged vows, her "I do" was smooth, weightless—like a line she'd rehearsed in private, never needing an audience. His was full of pride, spoken with conviction.

Juan sat in the back row. Silent. Watchful. He was the only one on her side of the aisle. But "family" wasn't the right word—Juan was the architect. Every brick, every license, every step leading her to the altar—he had designed it.

As the officiant declared them husband and wife, the guests burst into applause—ringing, bright, immediate. Laughter rippled through the crowd, and from that moment, the celebration truly began.

When Cassandra removed the veil herself—slowly, deliberately—it was like she'd waited her entire life to reveal her face in precisely that way, at precisely that moment. David saw only her eyes, glittering with what he thought was devotion. He felt chosen. Cherished. Reclaimed.

She hadn't made eye contact with Juan since he'd walked her down the aisle. But when the kiss ended and the applause swelled, they finally exchanged a glance — not romantic, not familial. A flicker of mutual knowing: efficient, coded, almost imperceptible. A quiet acknowledgment that they had just crossed another milestone in their plan.

But Reina caught it. So did David's mother. Not a glance—an exchange. Brief. Sharp. Surgical.

Reina turned to her mother. Their eyes met—wide, stunned, disbelieving. No words passed between them, but the look was enough. They had seen it. And they had seen each other see it. A quiet confirmation of what they'd feared, now made visible.

They didn't speak of it. But they knew what they'd seen.

Cassandra walked around the venue slowly. Not with hesitation, but with poise. Control. She didn't laugh during the toasts and made little to no eye contact with anyone not holding a camera.

She positioned herself near the lens, documenting the moment—not the marriage. She wasn't inhabiting the role. She was curating it.

By the time the chairs were stacked and the guests gone, she was still turned toward the lens. And David still turned toward her.

He couldn't take his eyes off her—mesmerized by her beauty, her charm, the way she seemed to glow in every room. It felt unreal, like life had handed him a second chance at love after so much loss. He watched her with quiet awe, almost in disbelief that someone like her had chosen someone like him. To David, she was a blessing—proof that love could return. To Cassandra, it was a breakthrough—the moment she stepped into the life she'd been building toward.

Reactions to the wedding had been mixed. Acquaintances offered congratulations. Friends voiced quiet concern. His siblings didn't speak to him for weeks. They didn't trust her. They'd tried to warn him, but he always said the same thing: "She's never given me a reason to doubt her."

All they had were instincts. He had what felt like evidence.

David remembered how it felt when he met Elena—that wordless certainty. The quiet click of recognition. Maybe love didn't need time. Just clarity. And Cassandra had presence. Warmth. Precision.

He trusted those feelings again, believing they would guide him toward something real. Believing that this—this moment, this woman, this choice—wasn't a mistake.

It was the beginning of something beautiful.

But beauty, he would learn, is sometimes just a façade.

CHAPTER 18

THE CHOREOGRAPHED WIFE

By the time the first anniversary approached, Cassandra had everything she wanted—access, admiration, and the illusion of intimacy. The performance had worked. But it hadn't happened overnight. It was earned—sweetly, precisely, and with the illusion of devotion.

For six months, David treated her like royalty. Cassandra responded with warmth and charm—affectionate, attentive, emotionally present. She painted their future in soft strokes: children, healing, holidays, retirement. A pretty picture, brushed with tenderness and promise.

To David, it wasn't just comforting—it was confirmation. Her sweetness felt like proof. He hadn't misjudged her. He hadn't rushed. He had simply opened himself to love again. And why wait, when it feels right?

In the months that followed, Cassandra played the doting wife to perfection—flawless, sly, choreographed to the last kiss. She cooked dinners, attended community events, smiled in all the right places. Every moment was staged to preserve the illusion of bliss.

She woke early, brewed his coffee, arranged breakfast like ceremony. Handed him vitamins. Kissed his cheek. "Just keeping my baby healthy," she'd say. The house gleamed—fresh linens, folded towels, his shirts pressed and sent to the dry cleaners—before he ever noticed. Dinner was always warm, plated, and waiting.

The perfect wife had laid the foundation. Now, the performance could begin—flawless, practiced, and designed not for affection, but for access.

She chose her moment with care: wine poured, music low, David too tired to notice the trap disguised as tenderness. That morning, he'd mentioned needing to review paperwork, and Cassandra had been ready—waiting for the opening.

The moment arrived wrapped in quiet vulnerability and domestic grace.

He came home late, briefcase heavy, mortgage documents spilling from the envelope. "It's going to be a long night," he sighed.

After dinner, Cassandra lingered beside him, her fingers tracing the rim of her wine glass. She didn't speak right away. Just leaned in slightly, her voice low and careful.

"Can I tell you something that's been on my mind?"

"Absolutely," he said. "I want us to have open communication. If something's troubling you, I want to know."

"David, I love our life together, and I'm grateful for everything you do," she said gently. "But sometimes I feel like I'm just... a decoration in your world. Something placed on the mantelpiece for show, then forgotten."

David reached for her hand, trying to steady the moment. "You're not forgotten. I don't know what I'd do without you."

He meant it. But he didn't quite understand what she was asking for—because it wasn't comfort she needed. It was access. And what she was really taking was control.

She shook her head gently. "You go back to meetings, phone calls, being needed. And I... I just wait. I want to build something too. I don't want to sit at home looking pretty—I want to be part of something. Part of your life."

There were no tears. Just precise vulnerability. Heavy enough to be felt. Light enough to be believed.

She rose and stepped toward the window, her silhouette framed by dusk. "I know people talk. I know your family hates me. But I'm not here to be ornamental." A pause. "I'm here to matter. I want to be an integral part of your world."

Something in David softened—not to the words, but to the ache they carried.

She returned to the sofa, folding herself beside him. "I'm already handling the errands, the laundry, meals... Maybe I could take on the finances too. That way your evenings aren't swallowed by paperwork— we'd have more time for us."

She didn't insist. She wrapped it in intimacy.

David looked at her, moved by the quiet pain behind the polish. "If you're willing," he said, "I'd love to let go of that piece."

She kissed his cheek. "Let me take care of it."

They opened joint accounts the following week.

To David, it was partnership. To Cassandra, it was access.

Two months in, Cassandra had proven herself flawless. The bills were paid early, the accounts balanced, the paperwork filed with precision. David no longer double-checked—he didn't need to. She was efficient, gracious, and quietly proud of the order she maintained.

To him, it felt like partnership. Like they were building something together—stable, intentional, lasting. He felt lucky. Relieved. Grateful.

That evening, tax forms spread across the coffee table. A rerun flickered silently on the TV.

"Baby," she said softly, tracing his wrist, "can I ask you something?"

"Sure."

"Since this house is only in your name... would I be able to stay here if something happened to you?"

David turned, unsure.

"I mean, we're planning to have children, and I'd have nowhere to go with the kids," she said, voice wrapped in possibility. "What would I do? No roof. No security."

She conjured it gently—diaper bags, laughter, Sunday mornings. Just enough for him to picture a future she'd never intend to live.

"I just want to make sure we'd be okay," she said. "That everything we're building is protected."

David paused, picturing the future she'd conjured—diaper bags, laughter, Sunday mornings. It felt real. It felt right.

He nodded. "You're right. We should add your name. It's your home too."

She nestled closer. "Thank you. That means everything."

To David, it felt like love. To Cassandra, it was the final key.

The signature was casual. A flick of the pen. But in that moment, the house became a vault she held the code to.

Predictable, cautious David—a man who had spent his adult life avoiding chaos—had walked straight into the arms of someone who choreographed it.

It was Mother's Day, and Reina had opened her home for a dinner party to honor their mother—and the other mothers among them.

The late afternoon light softened the edges of the living room, where bowls of fruit and trays of empanadas sat half-eaten on the table. Laughter floated in from the backyard—Junior at the grill, Luz chasing her niece through the garden. Inside, the mood was laid back, familiar. Teresa curled into the corner of the couch, Marisol poured sangria, and David stood near the fireplace, speaking with quiet pride.

"How's married life treating you both?" Teresa asked casually.

"Things have been great," David said. "Cassandra's brought a kind of rhythm to everything. We've synced up—finances, routines, even future plans."

He didn't boast, but there was a quiet satisfaction in his voice. As if marrying Cassandra had confirmed something he'd long hoped: that he could trust his instincts. That he'd chosen well.

Teresa smiled, tilting her glass. "Sounds like you've fully merged your lives."

David nodded. "And since it's Mother's Day, it feels like the right time to share—we're talking about kids. Taking steps. Hoping she'll be pregnant soon. Maybe next year we'll be celebrating for Cassandra too."

A pause followed—not awkward, but reflective.

Then Cassandra entered from the hallway, her presence light and composed. She carried a small plate of flan and set it gently on the table.

"Well," she said with a soft laugh, "we're not rushing anything. But yes—we're hopeful. We've talked about what kind of parents we want to be. What kind of home we want to build."

Marisol offered a warm smile. "That's a beautiful thing to plan for."

Reina glanced toward David, then back to Cassandra. "And your family? Will they be part of that picture?"

Cassandra's expression didn't falter, but her answer came carefully. "My family's... complicated. I'm close to my brother, Juan, but the rest—well, let's just say I've learned to build my own support system."

Luz nodded slowly. "That makes sense. Sometimes chosen family is the strongest kind."

David reached for Cassandra's hand. "She's already part of ours."

The room quieted—not in judgment, but in thought. These were the people who had seen David through heartbreak, through rebuilding. They weren't suspicious, but they were listening. Closely.

Junior stepped in from the patio, wiping his hands with a kitchen towel. "Well, if there's a baby on the way, I hope they inherit your stubborn streak, David. It's the only thing that kept you afloat some years." He grinned, then added, "Though let's hope they don't get your big nose. That thing's been leading the way since high school."

Laughter rippled through the room—easy, familiar. David rolled his eyes, but his smile lingered. Cassandra laughed too, the kind of laugh that blended in, smooth and practiced.

The moment passed—light, unspoken.

But Reina, slicing fruit at the counter, watched them both. She didn't interrupt. She didn't press. She simply listened—attuned to tone, timing, and the quiet truths that often live between words.

She and those closest to him weren't reassured. They were alarmed. Not by Cassandra's charm, but by how quickly David had given the store away—his trust, his assets, his guard.

Had he fallen in love—or into a trap?

Because Cassandra wasn't writing a new chapter. She was staging a long con.

Behind the scenes, she was orchestrating a full-scale financial heist. And David didn't know that the man visiting on weekends—the one she called her brother—wasn't her brother at all.

Cassandra was the social spark of the couple—a radiant host with just enough ambition to impress and just enough restraint to conceal. Early on, she'd told David she worked in real estate, and she made sure the detail held. She earned her license, affiliated with a local firm, and kept just enough paperwork on hand to make it official.

But it had little to do with selling homes. The credential wasn't a career—it was camouflage. A façade built to match the architecture of trust. A polished line for David's benefit. Something to point to when questions arose. A fallback excuse. A professional veneer to match the curated dinner parties and pristine countertops she maintained with ease.

Charm did the heavy lifting. She lit up rooms, closed deals with a smile, and whisked trays of holiday treats from the oven with enviable grace. Her calendar overflowed. Her flip phone buzzed constantly. To neighbors and guests, Cassandra was the portrait of balance and elegance—flawless, enviable, untouchable.

But admiration, David would soon learn, could be a kind of blindness. And lately, the light Cassandra cast felt colder.

It started quietly. She came home later, citing showings and meetings—all plausible. Her cell phone, one of those sleek, compact models agents favored, was always in her purse or clutched tightly. Calls were taken outside, her tone hushed, always brief.

Her laughter, once easy and sun-warmed, began to feel rehearsed. Her glances skimmed past David. Her touch lingered less.

The change was gradual but unmistakable—an emotional vanishing, not through anger but refinement.

Absence, curated.

She had learned to anticipate suspicion, manage scrutiny, and manipulate perception with surgical precision. Even David, who had once questioned small inconsistencies in their finances and her behavior, no longer dared to confront her. She had made confrontation feel like betrayal—his, not hers.

Cassandra took careful steps to isolate David emotionally and physically. She discouraged long hours with friends and family—those who might notice subtle shifts in her behavior or her growing influence over his time. Instead, she urged him to focus on work projects and community commitments, while she "handled things at home."

Keeping him busy with outside obligations ensured he had little time—or energy—to engage in financial affairs or household decisions. Her methods were quiet but corrosive—dissolving his support system before anyone noticed.

What looked like delegation was displacement. What felt like partnership was control.

Behind the scenes, her manipulation of the household and personal finances was meticulous. With an intimate knowledge of David's routines and habits, she carried out her plan with chilling efficiency. Quietly, she secured access to his assets, initiated transfers, and finalized arrangements that would cement her financial position.

And all the while, Cassandra remained the polished, public-facing figure of the con. Flawless. Enviable. Untouchable.

Beneath the veneer of the perfect wife, Cassandra was unraveling. The quiet rhythm of married life dulled her edges.

She craved luxury, attention, and the rush of being pursued. David's grounded nature—his routines, his loyalty—couldn't feed that appetite.

She missed the lounges, the parties, the fast life she once commanded. The thrill of being wanted. The power of being watched.

This wasn't a life. It was a role. And the costume was starting to itch.

The dinners, the folded towels, the staged affection—it all began to feel like confinement. A domestic charade. A slow suffocation.

She didn't know how long she could keep it up. But she knew one thing: cracking too soon would ruin the game. And Cassandra never folded early.

Still, the restlessness grew. She needed movement. Disruption. A way to breathe without breaking character.

That's when Juan began appearing more often. Always hovering at the edges. Always watching. He didn't ask questions. He didn't flinch at the performance. He understood the rules of the game.

His presence steadied her—reminded her of the life she'd once commanded. The thrill. The power. The precision.

She didn't know how long she could keep it up. But she knew that she had to be patient and wait for Juan to let her know when it was time and how to prepare for shifting the scene.

CHAPTER 19

THE THIRD WHEEL

Juan came often. Same knock. Same cologne. Always alone. And each time, the house felt a little less like David's. He never stayed long, but lingered just enough—for David to remember him, and never ask.

He moved through the space with practiced ease, like someone who'd studied every corner and every person beforehand. More than just "Cassandra's brother," Juan quietly managed things from behind the scenes—joking with David, offering help, his charm carefully measured, his presence constant yet oddly detached.

It didn't add up. For someone so familiar, Juan remained oddly unaccompanied—like a guest who never brought a life with him.

He was affable, warm, just distant enough. Never spoke of family. And Cassandra never introduced him by name—only as "my brother."

David assumed Juan—the brother from the wedding—was simply shy. But no one in David's family had ever seen him twice.

And Cassandra came alive around him. Her laugh stretched longer. Her tone softened. She straightened his tie more than once—intimate, instinctive, unnecessary.

David dismissed it at first. Dramatic family affection, he told himself. Loud. Effusive. Harmless. Until it wasn't.

One evening, Cassandra sat with Juan on the back patio, wine in hand, dusk settling like velvet. David had gone to bed early.

"I'm bored," she said, voice low but clear. "This life—it's too quiet. Too slow. I feel like I'm playing house."

Juan didn't respond right away. He just watched her, then said, "You need movement. You always have."

She exhaled, frustrated. "It's like I'm disappearing. Folding towels. Smiling on cue. I can't keep doing this."

Juan leaned back, swirling his wine. "I know it's taking time. But this kind of con—it needs polish. Precision. You're not just playing house. You're building the set. And when it's perfect, we take everything."

She nodded. "It would be easier if you were here. Not just visiting. Here."

Juan smiled. "Then make it happen."

She didn't answer. But the next evening, she did.

Cassandra asked David if Juan could move in. She said he had no other family in New York, was struggling, just needed somewhere to land while he found his footing.

David hesitated. Something in him resisted. But kindness had always been his compass. He wanted to believe that generosity could restore balance. That suspicion was just grief in disguise.

By then, Juan was already a fixture—half moved in emotionally, the way a builder moves in before the paint dries.

David agreed.

The night Juan moved in, the house held quiet. But the quiet no longer felt kind. It felt curated. Off.

On Juan's first night, he lingered after dinner. Folded his napkin with care. Leaned in across the table.

"David," he said, tone soft with sincerity, "I just want to say thank you. You're giving me a chance most people wouldn't. And Cassandra..." His eyes flicked toward her, lingering. "She's a force. You're lucky."

David smiled, but something inside him flinched.

The praise felt rehearsed.

Too practiced to be true.

After Juan moved in, Cassandra grew more distant. Her touch faded. Her laughter shortened. She no longer lingered in doorways or asked about David's day.

Yet she and Juan shared an intimacy that made David's stomach tighten. Their private smiles, those low exchanges laced with inside jokes he didn't understand, moved like a private language—a rhythm too practiced to be coincidental.

As Cassandra withdrew, Juan grew more familiar. He moved through the house like a resident, not a guest. Juan had evolved—from guest to fixture, from fixture to something more insidious.

Behind the scenes, he operated in the shadows—the architect of infrastructure: setting up shell companies, digital footprints, contingency plans. Together, they formed a dual system. Cassandra charmed. Juan calculated. She managed perception. He managed logistics.

But it wasn't just the logistics. It was the way Juan looked at David—like he was studying a pattern, not a person. His gaze was clinical, almost bored. Not hostile. Not mocking. Just detached. As if David were a variable in a long equation, and Juan had already solved for the outcome.

One morning, David heard him whispering on the kitchen phone: "Yeah. He's still clueless... No, she's working on it. Couple more months, maybe less."

The voice was casual. Cruel in its confidence.

David stepped into the room. Juan turned, smile intact. "Morning, boss. You need coffee?"

David nodded, but something in him recoiled. He wasn't sure what Juan meant—what "she's working on" or who "he" referred to—but the tone chilled him. It wasn't just the words. It was the ease. The entitlement. The manner in which Juan spoke—with the casual confidence of someone who'd already won.

Each time David returned—whether from business trips, the office, or even just stepping away to the next room—he noticed their rhythm had deepened. The familiarity between them felt rehearsed, as if carefully practiced during his absence. Though David had entrusted them with his confidence, he now found himself quietly excluded from something unfolding just beyond his reach.

Once, he stepped into the kitchen and found them standing close. Not affectionate. But proximate in a way that felt coded. Cassandra adjusted her blouse. Juan glanced away. David felt like an intruder in his own home. The moment vanished, but unease lingered.

One night, David woke to find the bed empty. He stepped into the hallway, his heart slow and heavy. He heard voices—low, intimate—behind the guest room door. Cassandra's laugh came first. Then Juan: "It's almost time."

David didn't speak. He returned to bed, swallowed the quiet, and let bitterness root itself deep.

From then on, the word brother tasted spoiled. It wasn't kinship—it was camouflage. A smokescreen. A misdirection.

David didn't know anything for certain—not yet. But something in their rhythm felt off. Too familiar. Too rehearsed. His mind hadn't found proof. But his instincts had begun to whisper.

CHAPTER 20

THE DRAFT UNDER THE DOOR

It was the incident in the study that finally broke him.

David had come home early—earlier than expected—and found Juan standing at his desk, fingers grazing sealed envelopes.

Juan turned casually, smile intact. "Just looking for a pen," he said.

David nodded, silent. But the drawer with the pens wasn't open. And something in him shifted.

But the drawer with the pens wasn't open.

David nodded, silent. But something in him shifted. It wasn't just the intrusion. It was the ease. The assumption. The way Juan moved through the house like it belonged to him.

That night, David couldn't sleep. Cassandra curled beside him—warm, familiar, perfectly placed. But her presence felt staged. And Juan's touch on the envelopes—so casual, so precise—kept replaying in his mind.

He got up, walked to the kitchen, poured a glass of water, and stood in the quiet. The house felt staged. Even the silence had a script.

He could've called Junior. They'd been through enough together—loss, recovery, the long road back. But this wasn't grief. It wasn't a crisis. It was something quieter. Slipperier. And for that, he needed someone like Marisol.

She had an excellent bullshit meter. And she'd help him understand what was happening in his own home—especially the parts he couldn't yet articulate.

He didn't call her that night. But the next morning, he did.

His voice trembled. "I don't know what's happening," he said. "It's like they're choreographing my life. Juan is everywhere. Cassandra deflects everything. I feel like I'm living in a set someone else built."

Marisol listened, quiet for a moment. Then: "David, I don't know exactly what's going on. But I do know this—your instincts are trying to tell you something. And you need to listen."

David laughed—soft, nervous. "I keep telling myself it's just family closeness. That I'm being paranoid."

"You're not being paranoid," she said gently. "You're being perceptive. There's a difference. When something feels off, it usually is. Maybe not dramatically so. Maybe not dangerous. But off."

She paused, then added, "And David—siblings can be close, sure. But this kind of closeness? No boundaries, no backstory, no one else in the picture? That's not just unusual. That's curated."

He didn't respond right away.

"I've seen this before," she continued. "Not this exact setup, but the pattern. People who don't fall in love—they fall into roles. They rehearse connection until it looks real. And if you're not careful, you start mistaking performance for intimacy."

David exhaled, slow. "So what do I do?"

"Don't accuse. Don't confront. Just pay attention. Watch for what's consistent—and what's curated. Look at how they respond when you're off-script. When you ask questions they didn't expect."

Her voice softened. "You don't have to decide anything tonight."

"Just don't ignore the draft under the door," she said. "It's there for a reason."

Her words settled like static beneath his ribs.

Not loud. But impossible to ignore.

David's unease continued to grow. There was something wrong, but he couldn't name it.

Taking heed of Marisol's advice, he said nothing. Silence felt safer than accusation.

At neighborhood gatherings, Cassandra and David still held hands and smiled. No one suspected a fracture. Juan played the charming sidekick, always conveniently placed, always casually involved. Their smiles were props. Their bond was a stage set. No one looked behind it. No one saw David studying his wife like a stranger.

David watched. Waited. Moments replayed themselves in his head, warped by hindsight—an eerie smile, a laugh that died too quickly, a touch that felt more performance than affection. Weekends hollowed. Errands turned solitary. Cassandra disappeared for tours that bled into evenings. No shouting. No slammed doors. Just absence—measured and growing.

It didn't feel like the wear and tear of routine. It felt like displacement.

So David became methodical. Not just logging calendar entries, but cross-referencing them with receipts, mileage, and timestamps.

He created a spreadsheet—color-coded, meticulous. Like everything else in his life.

It wasn't just data. It was proof he hadn't imagined the erosion.

One Saturday, Cassandra left early for what she described as a house showing with an out-of-town buyer. She kissed David lightly, her lips barely brushing his cheek, and vanished.

Later, when he called the agency's office line, her name wasn't listed. Not for that client. Not for that day.

Something bloomed inside him—an ache edged with clarity. Still, he didn't confront. Not yet. Asking meant naming it. Naming it made it real. And real wasn't something he was ready to acknowledge.

She stepped outside for most conversations or locked the bathroom door. David noticed inconsistencies—appointments that didn't exist, errands that stretched too long, explanations that felt rehearsed. The office line never confirmed her presence. Her excuses began to fray. At home, the performance unraveled.

David, wanting to take control of his household, sat with Cassandra on the patio, watching dusk settle like dust.

"I've been thinking," he said, his tone even, deliberate. "It's been three months. When is Juan leaving?"

Cassandra looked up, folding a towel with practiced ease. "He's still figuring things out," she said. "You know how hard it is—we're the only family he has in New York. No stability. He's trying."

David nodded slowly. "I know. But he's... everywhere. The kitchen. The study. The guest room. I feel like I'm the one visiting."

She smiled gently, disarming. "You're not. This is your home. Ours. Juan's just grateful. He's trying not to be a burden."

David hesitated. "I'm not sure he knows what a burden looks like."

Cassandra didn't respond right away. She smoothed the towel, precise, deliberate.

David's voice dropped. "He may be trying, but not hard enough. I want our privacy back—our space. Just you and me. How are we supposed to start a family with your brother always in the middle of everything?"

She looked up, her expression unreadable. Then laughed softly, brushing a wrinkle from the towel. "You're tired. Work's been nonstop. Let me talk to him. Maybe it's time we set a timeline."

"Soon," David said. "Please."

Later that night, Cassandra entered the guest room. Juan was at the desk, typing. "He asked when you're leaving," she said. Juan didn't look up. "Did he sound serious?" "He's getting impatient," she replied. "He wants space. He wants me back." Juan stopped typing. "Then we accelerate." "He's watching now," Cassandra said quietly. "Not just wondering. Watching." Juan smiled. "Let him. The transfers have already started."

She hesitated. "We might need more time. Three months, maybe six. That would put us at a year and a half. Enough to finish clean." Juan considered. "If he pushes harder, we'll have to move faster. But if you can stall—just a little—we can finish the sweep without noise."

The con had shape now. Not suspicion—blueprint. David's assets had been mapped. Retirement accounts flagged. Authorizations quietly processed. The first transfers had begun—small enough to avoid alarms, precise enough to matter.

In the meantime, Cassandra played for time. She deflected David's requests, softened her tone, offered reassurances. Said Juan just needed a few more months. That she was helping him get settled. All the while, she maintained the choreography of the perfect wife—meticulous in the house, attentive in the details, steady in the role. She kissed David's cheek. She kept the performance alive—just long enough to finish the job.

David's suspicion didn't arrive all at once. The first crack didn't explode—it whispered.

He had learned something: silence could be cultivated. Trust could be dismantled in perfect stillness. Betrayal didn't arrive with fireworks. It simmered—quiet as folded laundry. Sharp as a lipstick stain where none should be.

He thought of Elena—the weight of her absence, now six years distant. Their love had been quieter, steadier. Even their silences had structure. They were architectural. Intentional. Built from trust, not concealment.

What he felt with Cassandra wasn't silence. It was erasure. And it carried the shape of something designed. Not accidental. Not emotional. Engineered. The contrast haunted him—not because Cassandra failed to be Elena, but because her presence felt like a performance. And he was no longer sure who the audience was.

He didn't know exactly what he was looking for. Only that something felt off—too polished, too rehearsed. He didn't know when the truth would surface, or what shape it might take.

But he knew one thing: the answers wouldn't come from Cassandra's lips. She was too careful now. Too curated.

So David turned to the one thing that had never lied to him—numbers. They were neutral. Precise. Unemotional.

He didn't expect confirmation. Just clarity.

A place to begin tracing what his instincts already knew but couldn't yet name.

The draft was still there. And now, he was listening.

CHAPTER 21

WHEN THE VEIL FELL

Sixteen months in, the veil began to slip. David's instincts had sharpened—not just about Cassandra, but about her so-called brother. The charm had thinned. The orchestration was fraying. And now, alone in a hotel room on a business trip, he stopped pretending not to notice the quiet itch in his chest.

He started with the numbers.

He hadn't checked his finances in nearly three months. And now that he thought about it, he hadn't seen a single monthly statement. Cassandra handled the mail. She managed the household accounts. What had once been a weekly ritual—reviewing balances, tracking expenses—had quietly shifted into her domain. Not from neglect, but from trust.

She was meticulous. David, buried in consulting deadlines and lulled by her precision, had let go gradually. The account was their shared vessel. And somewhere along the way, he had stopped looking.

Small withdrawals, dressed as routine transfers, never broke the surface. Not enough to trigger alarms. Not enough to disturb the illusion.

But tonight, something tugged. A flicker of unease. He logged in casually, almost out of habit.

The glow of his laptop cast long shadows across the carpet. He opened his Merrill Lynch account—the interface sluggish, still oddly futuristic. It was the first time he'd checked it in over three months.

Then everything fractured.

$602,000.

He blinked. Refreshed the page. Blinked again.

That couldn't be right. The account—his main savings—should've held over $1.2 million.

His pulse quickened. He reached for the phone and dialed Merrill Lynch.

"Michael Stevens," came the familiar voice.

"Michael, it's David Ortiz. I just checked my account, and the balance is... wrong. Can you pull up the last six months of activity?"

"Of course. One moment."

David paced the room, heart thudding. He heard the clack of keys on the other end—familiar, mechanical, steady.

"Okay, I'm in," Michael said.

David sat down again, the soft hum of filtered air surrounding him. Rain tapped against the windows, steady and indifferent.

"I need you to walk me through the transactions."

Michael scanned the ledger.

"Forty-nine transfers," he said. "Each just under ten thousand. Totaling $490,200. Routed through different vendors—none repeated. And most of them don't even look real."

Michael frowned. "Thing is, these transfers didn't go through Merrill's internal systems. They were client-directed, routed externally. On paper, they look like routine disbursements. No single one raises a flag—but together? It's a mosaic of misdirection."

He looked up, eyes narrowing. "This isn't sloppy bookkeeping. It's a pattern. Someone went out of their way to keep it quiet."

David leaned forward. The screen glowed with names he barely recognized.

Pine Hollow Interiors. A wallpaper consultation that never happened. Five thousand wired. Legitimate on paper. Forgettable in memory.

Linden & Shaw. Supposed landscapers. $9,800 gone under "spring improvements." The invoice was pristine—mulch weight, labor hours, fertilizer specs. He'd signed off, distracted by a deadline, trusting Cassandra's explanation.

Michael continued, voice steady. "Most of the transfers were processed late at night.

The invoices look real—typed, itemized, even stamped—but they're fabricated. The vendor names trace back to shell companies. Southern Sun Ltd., Golden Arc Partners, C&J Consulting. All registered to P.O. boxes. No verified business licenses. No tax IDs."

He paused. "David, from what I can see, the withdrawals weren't dramatic. They were deliberate."

David didn't speak. He stared at the screen, the pattern emerging—quiet, precise, designed to stay invisible.

Michael clicked into the final transaction. "Three weeks ago. $88,000. Marked as Cottage Restoration."

David's breath caught. "She was in Vermont," he said quietly. "Alone."

Michael nodded. "The wire was split across three accounts—Panama, George Town, and a boutique trust tied to a Catskill property. The routing of funds was layered. Someone knew what they were doing."

David's voice was low, almost reluctant. "Cassandra?"

"She authorized the transfers," Michael said. "But the setup—the shell companies, the invoices, the routing—this points to coordination. It's not amateur work. It's structured. Professional."

David stared at the screen. The betrayal wasn't emotional. It was architectural. Mapped in spreadsheets. Backed by documents. Clean fonts. Precise dates. Measured theft.

"All the transfers," Michael added, "were processed under Cassandra's credentials. No internal flags. Everything matched—amounts, dates, vendor names. It was built to pass."

David's stomach turned. "Do any of these vendors exist?"

"Not in our system. No licenses. No filings. Just names."

Michael's voice cut through the silence. "We've tallied the total. Across all vendors, all transfers—authorized under Cassandra's credentials. It comes to $598,000, including fees, currency conversions, and routing costs." He paused. "That confirms your current balance of $602,000."

David didn't speak.

The room held its quiet. He exhaled—slowly, deliberately. The glow of the screen reflected back at him, sterile and unforgiving.

On the other end, Michael hesitated. "David? Are you there? Are you okay?"

David swallowed. His voice was low, steady, but distant. "Yes. I'm here, Michael. Thank you for the information."

Michael's tone softened. "Let me know if you need anything else. We're here to help."

A beat passed.

"Thank you. I'll follow up with Cassandra."

David stared at the screen. The numbers didn't lie. But the truth—the real truth—had been buried beneath layers of silence and deception, hidden just out of reach.

Michael's voice faded into the background. The numbers were damning. But they weren't the only betrayal.

David hadn't imagined fraud. Not really. Not until now. But Michael had confirmed it—quietly, precisely. And that precision unsettled him most.

It wasn't just the money. It was the patience. The choreography. The betrayal. His account hadn't been emptied by accident. It had been drained with elegance.

He thought back to the first time Cassandra offered to manage the finances. —It'll be easier —she'd said. One login. One system. I'll handle the details. Less than a year into their marriage, she was managing utilities, handling insurance claims, even filing their taxes. Her access had expanded gradually—full-spectrum, organic, invisible.

Now he understood why. She hadn't wanted simplicity. She'd wanted control.

The betrayal wasn't loud. It was mapped in spreadsheets, not tears. Backed by documents, not confession. Clean fonts. Precise dates. Measured theft.

But the numbers weren't the only deception.

He thought of the way Cassandra adjusted Juan's collar. The way her laughter stretched longer when he was near. The glances that lingered. The silences that felt rehearsed. It hadn't looked like theft. It had looked like something else. Too intimate. Too familiar. Not familial.

He'd wondered, once or twice, if there was something between them—something unspoken, maybe even physical. But he'd buried it. Told himself it was dramatic. Paranoid.

Now, though, the financial precision reframed everything. The glances. The silences. The practiced proximity. It wasn't just plausible—it was probable. And he couldn't help but wonder: how deep did their relationship really go?

The money was gone. But something deeper had been taken—trust, clarity, the quiet belief that love had been the point.

At almost forty, David was the portrait of intentional living. His home in upstate New York bore the evidence—spreadsheets color-coded and bookmarked, investment records organized to the decimal. He had begun saving in his twenties, watching the account grow through grit and strategic restraint. His dream was simple: retire early, travel the world, checking off each destination with the same quiet joy he applied to his financial planning.

Her death left a void, but not despair. Between their shared savings and the benefits from her life insurance, 401(k), and Mobil package, David had been left with $2.5 million—more than enough to ensure he'd never struggle.

Cassandra Jiménez seemed, for a time, to be the future incarnate: magnetic, intuitive, admired. Their love story was so convincing that even the skeptical neighbors softened. But beauty can be weaponized. And the cruelest betrayals come wrapped in charm. She knew his strengths. More importantly, she knew what would hurt most.

It wasn't just financial. It was existential.

On that March morning, rain stitched quiet patterns across cobblestone streets. David's hand trembled slightly as he closed the laptop.

He canceled the rest of his trip—no client dinners, no conference panels. He booked the next flight home without alerting Cassandra. Not out of vengeance, but because explanations felt premature. He needed to see the house. The files. The floorboards. The expressions.

He thought he was ready.

But the truth waiting for him wasn't just calculated. It was intimate.

And when the veil finally fell, it didn't flutter—it cut.

CHAPTER 22

TRUTH EXPOSED

They hadn't expected him home for another three days.

But betrayal doesn't wait for timing—it waits for silence.

David arrived just after five. The house didn't greet him—it recoiled. Too quiet. Too arranged. Not the hush of solitude, but the kind of silence that knows it's guilty. The air felt wrong. The temperature off. A familiar space suddenly foreign.

Then he heard it—laughter. Light. Intimate. Drifting from the master bedroom.

His breath caught. His heart slammed against his ribs, as though it already knew the truth his mind refused to name. Slowly, he placed his keys on the counter. As he climbed the stairs, he was careful to step on the outer edges of each step, where the floorboards were sturdier and less likely to creak as did not want to alert them.

The bedroom door was ajar.

David approached slowly, his breath shallow, his steps deliberate. He didn't want to be heard—not yet. This wasn't confrontation. It was reconnaissance. Confirmation. A quiet reckoning before the storm.

He eased the door open, careful not to let it creak.

What he saw shattered his world—the moment suspicion hardened into certainty.

Cassandra and Juan lay tangled in the sheets. Bare skin. Unbothered ease. No panic. No shame. Just intimacy.

His gaze swept the room: clothes strewn across the floor, sheets twisted in betrayal, the air thick with sweat and perfume. For a moment, David couldn't process it. His mind stalled, senses misfiring, reality refusing to make sense. Cassandra and her brother? The image defied logic. He had to recalibrate—sight, sound, meaning. It was as if his body registered the betrayal before his brain could name it.

Then came the surge. His first instinct was pure violence.

Not metaphorical. Not restrained. He wanted to break something.

To leave a mark. To make the moment unforgettable—not just for them, but for himself. His vision narrowed. Breath stalled. The heat bloomed behind his eyes—a fury so sharp it cracked logic. He stepped forward, every muscle primed to swing, to destroy, to make their betrayal unforgettable.

But something stopped him.

It wasn't restraint—it was a return. Not to calm, but to clarity. A blackout, brief but binding. Some part of him—maybe Elena's grace, maybe his own decency—stepped in and whispered: not this.

So he stood. And watched. Not because he lacked rage. But because grace—disguised as a whisper—held him at the edge and refused to let him tip.

They didn't notice him.

Cassandra and Juan were too consumed—too entangled in each other, in their laughter, in the ease of betrayal—to sense the figure standing just beyond the threshold. David's presence was silent, deliberate, invisible. He let the moment stretch, let the truth settle in its rawest form.

Then, without a word, he kicked the door wide open.

The slam echoed through the room like a gunshot. It wasn't an attack—it was punctuation. A declaration. A warning. The force of it made the walls shudder.

Cassandra gasped, clutching the sheet to her chest. Juan scrambled upright, reaching for his pants, eyes wide, breath caught. They had been oblivious to David's presence—but now they were exposed. Scrambling. Stunned. Guilty.

David didn't speak. He didn't need to. His presence was no longer passive. It was undeniable. He let them see it—the fury, the betrayal, the full weight of what they'd done.

Then, he turned and walked out.

Behind him, the silence fractured. Cassandra pulled the sheet tighter, her breath shallow. Juan muttered something—low, defensive, panicked.

After David walked away, they didn't follow. Instead, they stayed in the room, scrambling to put clothes on, their ears straining to catch any sign of his next move.

Uncertain what was coming, they remained in the bedroom—stunned, exposed, waiting.

Outside, the wind was colder than forecasted. David didn't pace or swear. He didn't cry. He inhaled—slow, deliberate—as if anchoring himself in the shape of what came next. Then he dialed 911.

His voice, when it came, was low. Controlled. But not calm. There was a tremor beneath the precision, a tightness that made the words land heavy. "I need to report a domestic fraud," he said. "And trespassing."

A pause. Then the operator's voice, alert but gentle: "Sir, are you in a safe location?"

"I'm outside," David said. "I'm not hurt. But I need this documented. I need it recorded. The address is 14 Sycamore Lane, Cold Spring. I want officers dispatched. I want the trespassers removed from my property."

Her tone shifted. "Understood. Officers are on their way. Please remain where you are. Do not go back into the house."

He stood beneath the streetlight, the ache inside him palpable. Not rage. Not panic. Just the sharp clarity of a man who had finally seen the full shape of the deception—and was ready to respond.

And then the situation crystallized. The wire transfers. The fake authorizations. The shell companies. It was all connected. Cassandra hadn't betrayed him just with her body—she'd dismantled his life in silence.

Shock gave way to clarity—the kind that doesn't shout, but steadies. He wasn't broken. He was awake.

Now everything made sense. The intimacy between them had never been familial. It had been coded. Practiced. Performed. This wasn't a mistake. It was deliberate.

David felt the sting of humiliation, but it didn't consume him. The pain was sharp—yes—but it was also instructive. He wasn't just hurt. He was resolute. He wouldn't rage. He wouldn't beg. He wouldn't unravel.

He would respond. With precision. With truth. With everything they hadn't expected.

He wasn't going to sweep this under the carpet or nurse his wounds in private. He was going to fight back. Not just for himself—but to expose them. To make sure the damage they'd done didn't stay hidden.

As the full realization settled, David spoke again to the operator. His voice was steady, stripped of softness. "I'm going back inside," he said. "I'll keep the line open."

"I want the record to begin at the moment of truth," he said.

"Not the moment of rage."

The operator advised against it, her tone urgent, caution layered beneath protocol. But David was already moving—deliberate, composed, unshaken. He wasn't returning for vengeance. He was returning for resolution.

David reentered the house with the phone still in his hand, the line open, recording everything. He wasn't calm, but he was composed—held together by the thin thread of purpose. The police were en route. That knowledge steadied him. It gave him structure. It gave him time. More importantly, it gave him distance—from impulse, from escalation, from the kind of violence that Juan might provoke.

He crossed the threshold not for vengeance, but for truth. And truth, he now understood, had a rhythm of its own.

Inside, the room was quiet—but not still. Then came the sound of footsteps—measured, deliberate—approaching from the hallway. Juan and Cassandra turned toward the door in unison. He straightened, instinctively bracing for confrontation. She was crouched by the dresser, stuffing clothes into a duffel with mechanical urgency, her posture tense, eyes flickering with unease.

Cassandra had moved quickly after David left, not to hide—but to prepare. Her gasp had come late, as if delayed by calculation. Juan's scramble had been quick but uncertain, more reflex than panic. Neither spoke. The silence thickened, heavy with exposure.

David didn't return to the bedroom quietly. His footsteps were heavy, and he entered with a bang—kicking the door open hard enough to make the frame shudder. It wasn't carelessness. It was intention. He didn't want to be gentle. He wanted them to feel the force, the fury, the rupture. The sound ricocheted through the room like a warning shot, sharp and final.

Juan flinched, instinctively rising from the recliner. Cassandra froze mid-motion, one hand still gripping the zipper of the duffel. They turned toward him, not with surprise, but with recognition. They knew what this was.

David stepped into the room, his presence unmistakable. He didn't speak right away. He let the silence stretch, let the weight of the moment settle like dust after impact.

Then, his voice—low, steady, stripped of affection.

"He's not your brother," he said, eyes locked on Cassandra.

She didn't answer. Juan held his breath.

David didn't move closer. He didn't raise his voice. But the receiver was still warm in his hand, the line open, the soft hum of connection audible. Every word was being recorded. He wanted it documented—not just the fraud, but the intimacy, the planning, the betrayal.

This wasn't a confrontation. It was a reckoning.

His eyes stayed on Cassandra, and something in his expression hardened.

"You didn't bring him here out of pity or obligation," he said quietly. "You brought him into my home to help you bleed it dry."

Cassandra didn't flinch, but her grip on the duffle bag tightened.

"You let me believe he was family," David said, his voice rising just enough to cut through the silence. "You sat across from me at dinner. You smiled. All the while, you were both conspiring against me in the guest room."

He paused, the weight of the moment settling.

"When I walked into this house, I was ready to confront you about the money. That was the plan—the theft, the shell companies, the quiet siphoning of my life. But I wasn't ready for this. For my wife to be in bed with her so-called brother. For the betrayal to be not just strategic, but intimate. And now, I don't know which is worse—the relationship or the theft. One gutted my accounts. The other gutted the truth."

"This morning I spoke with the broker," David continued. "The total siphoned from my account is just under six hundred thousand dollars. Every transaction traced. Every shell company named."

He turned to Juan. "This wasn't one reckless transfer. It was dozens—small enough not to raise alarms. You dripped the betrayal in increments. Every wire approved. Every login traceable. I gave Cassandra full access."

"You didn't just steal," David said. "You counted on my trust to hide it. You knew my patterns. My habits. You knew exactly what wouldn't trigger alerts—what I wouldn't notice until it was too late."

A beat passed. Cassandra's fingers curled tighter around the duffle bag. Juan swallowed hard. Then Cassandra blinked—the first crack in her composure. Not remorse. Fear.

Juan stood abruptly. "Good luck getting that money back. It's gone. Split. Buried."

David didn't blink.

"Then I'll dig," he said. "And I'll drag your names through every court, every audit, every deposition until the last dollar is accounted for. You didn't just rob me—you underestimated me."

Cassandra's voice sharpened. "You're bluffing. You don't have the intestinal fortitude to withstand the kind of investigation this would trigger. You'd be exposing yourself to the world as a fool."

David stepped closer, the receiver still pressed to his palm. "I didn't have the intestinal fortitude, as you say, for betrayal. But I've found it—for justice."

Cassandra stood and took a step closer to David. "I loved you. Maybe not how you wanted. But I did—in my way."

David didn't respond right away. He let the words hang—empty, rehearsed, already too late.

David shook his head. "No. You loved access. You loved control. You loved the silence I kept while you hollowed me out."

"You never noticed," Cassandra said quietly. "Not the money missing. Not me."

David cut in, his voice steady. "It's not that I didn't notice. It's that I trusted you to do the right thing. But you're right about one thing—I never saw through the mask you wore, or your performance as the perfect wife."

Cassandra stared at him, her expression unreadable. "I know how you breathe," she whispered. "How you sleep. How you hesitate before locking the door."

David blinked once. "You studied me like a safe."

Juan let out a dry laugh. "You were easy. Predictable. You made it simple."

David's gaze didn't waver. "Thank you for confessing," he said.

Then, calmly, he spoke into the receiver still pressed to his palm. "I hope you got all of that."

A voice responded, crisp and steady. "Yes, sir. Everything's been recorded."

"Please stay on the line until the officers arrive."

"I will. Thank you."

Cassandra and Juan froze. "What?"

David lifted the handset slightly, letting them hear the faint hum of the open line. "The call's been live this entire time. Dispatch heard everything. I'll be requesting the transcript."

Cassandra's face drained of color. Juan stepped back.

"You tricked us."

"No," David said.

"You exposed yourselves."

He turned toward the entryway, voice quiet but final. "I will pursue this to the fullest extent of the law—civil, criminal, federal. You have ten minutes to leave before the officers arrive."

The receiver buzzed faintly in his hand. Dispatch was still listening.

Juan cursed. Cassandra didn't speak.

David didn't flinch. He walked out, the line still humming softly. He didn't look back.

Chaos unfolded in the bedroom—a rupture sealed by David's confirmation that their confession had just been relayed to the 911 operator.

Cassandra scrambled to finish packing. Juan shoved traveler's checks, a spiral ledger, and loose cash into their emergency tote—jaw clenched, movements clipped. There was no hesitation, only practiced speed. They moved like operatives executing a contingency plan they never truly believed they'd need.

Cassandra's hands shook as she scanned the room for anything they'd missed. Juan didn't flinch. His movements were precise, methodical—nerves of steel honed by repetition. The exposure was complete. Not just discovered—documented. And unlike their other targets, David wasn't ashamed. He wasn't retreating. He was pressing charges.

Juan cursed, voice low and bitter. "We were almost there—just a few more days."

"I know," she snapped. "We were days away from a clean exit. One last transfer and we'd have the full $1.2 million."

That final transfer had been the coup de grâce. They hadn't cared if it triggered alarms—they'd planned to be long gone before anyone noticed. But David had come home early. Unannounced. Surgical.

"He's not yelling," she added, dragging on a coat. "Which means he's calculating."

They hadn't rehearsed it often—but enough to be ready. Cassandra had mapped the exit routes. Juan had memorized the financial transfers. Together, they'd built the shell companies, scrubbed the metadata, timed the withdrawals. They were professionals.

The one thing they hadn't prepared for was resistance.

In all their previous cons, men like David didn't fight back. They folded. They disappeared. They walked away in shame—too stunned or humiliated to pursue justice.

"He's not like the others," Juan said, voice tight. "They fold. They vanish. He's going to drag this out."

Cassandra's face was pale, eyes darting. "We underestimated him."

This wasn't just another exit. This was collapse.

David hadn't followed the script. He hadn't swallowed the shame or retreated into silence. He hadn't frozen. He'd fought. And now, for the first time in their criminal career, Cassandra and Juan weren't just exposed—they were being held to account.

There were no arguments. No blame passed between them. The collapse was mutual—and irreversible.

Only escape.

In under fifteen minutes, they were gone—slipping out the back door, hoping to avoid the flashing lights and questions already on their way. Their exit, once calculated and clean, now felt like flight. Not from justice. But from the one mark who refused to stay silent.

David stepped outside. The wind pressed against his collar as he stood beneath the streetlight, the ache inside him surgical. Precise. Clean. The house behind him felt hollow now, stripped of meaning. He hadn't seen them leave, but he saw Cassandra's car vanish down the road followed by Juan's.

Neighbors later recalled the blur of her car rocketing down the driveway, tires skimming gravel. Juan in his car wearing sunglasses despite the rain—shielding his eyes, perhaps, not from weather, but from consequence.

David stayed on the line with the 911 operator just long enough to confirm their exit. Then, calmly, he told the dispatcher they had fled—and that he would wait for the officers inside.

He had waited outside until they were gone. He hadn't wanted to share space with them—hadn't wanted to breathe the same air. He needed distance—from the betrayal, from the rot.

CHAPTER 23

UNRAVELING THE CON

David didn't reenter the house as a husband. He reentered as a witness.

Not of love lost—but of a life repurposed.

In the minutes after Cassandra and Juan fled, he drifted through the rooms like someone tracing the outline of a wound. The betrayal was fresh—raw, architectural. Not just infidelity, but infrastructure.

The silence met him like a second betrayal—familiar but stripped of illusion. Every object felt suspect. Every room, a ledger. He didn't flinch. He didn't mourn. He moved with the precision of someone who had stopped asking why and started asking how.

Wine glasses still sweated with the residue of their intimacy. The closet stood bare—a silent witness to their retreat. Cassandra's laptop glowed like a confession, its thick frame humming faintly, the screen lit with evidence.

He moved through the house like a man tracing the edges of a crime scene—his own life, cordoned and gutted. The silence wasn't just absence. It was aftermath. A bruise in the air, still tender.

He began to catalog—not just what was missing, but what had been weaponized.

He didn't sit. Stillness felt complicit.

The house hadn't been ransacked. It had been repurposed. Every drawer, every login, every glance had been part of the performance. And he had been the audience—unaware, trusting, blind.

His breath was steady, but his pulse was sharp. He didn't scream. He didn't collapse. He printed flagged transactions, traced the shell company, and made a note to contact his accountant.

The betrayal clung to the walls like smoke. The silence wasn't peace—it was participation. Every surface had absorbed the lie.

But it no longer claimed him.

David stood in the quiet, no longer trying to make sense of it. The illusion had shattered. The trust, the shared purpose, the love weaponized as leverage—it had all collapsed. What remained was clarity. And resolve.

He stood by the window, shoulders squared. He wasn't watching for their return. He was tracing the shape of their absence.

They hadn't reacted to confrontation. They had reacted to exposure.

Officer Diana Ramirez stepped into the foyer around 6:50 p.m., boots damp from the rain, eyes narrowing on two half-full wine glasses and the faint glow of a screen still active in the kitchen. No broken windows. No raised voices. Cassandra and Juan were already gone. Their exit was swift and clinical.

She didn't speak. She didn't need to. She wasn't reading a crime scene; she was reading psychology. Minds that had vacuum-sealed their emotions and left only trace elements behind. This wasn't panic. It was the tail end of something carefully rehearsed.

Ramirez didn't find chaos. She found choreography.

Not aftermath. Architecture.

The house was quiet. No motion. Just the low hum of a laptop glowing on the kitchen counter—screen still open to a ledger. And there, in the center of the silence, stood a man who had been betrayed, belittled, underestimated—but refused to be dismantled.

Seasoned and intuitive, Ramirez moved through the house like a litmus test, quietly absorbing the atmosphere. The silence felt engineered. David's hands trembled as he pointed to the screen. The numbers didn't lie. Neither did his eyes.

But it wasn't the silence that unsettled her. It was how perfectly it had been staged. The betrayal hadn't just happened. It had been rehearsed.

Detective Carmela Mendez arrived less than an hour later with a small team and a briefcase full of quiet relentlessness. Sharp-featured and surgically observant, she moved through the house like someone charting the collapse of a façade in slow motion.

David met her in the hallway, composed but alert. "She left in a hurry," he said, voice low. "I told her she had ten minutes before the officers arrived. She grabbed what she could—but she forgot something."

He gestured toward the kitchen. "Her laptop. It's still open. The ledger's on the screen."

Mendez followed his gaze. The glow from the counter was quiet but damning—a confession in pixels.

David handed over contracts, login histories, flagged transactions. He printed and gave them the report of the transfers he'd received from his broker at Merrill Lynch. No dramatics. Just clarity. Just war.

Within the hour, the living room became a staging ground—legal pads lining the coffee table, bank statements, property records. David's war room blurred into the investigation's blueprint.

"Have you filed anything offshore?" Mendez asked.

David nodded. "Three accounts—Belize, the British Virgin Islands, and a quiet trust. All legal. All documented. Cassandra never touched them."

Years earlier, David had taken steps to protect his assets by setting up financial accounts outside the United States—in countries known for strong privacy laws and favorable tax structures. These offshore accounts weren't secret. They were strategic. Registered properly. Compliant with international regulations. Structured for long-term security.

Cassandra had access to their shared domestic accounts—the ones used for household expenses and joint investments. But the offshore accounts were different. They were in David's name only, with layers of protection she couldn't bypass. Access required legal credentials, multi-step verification, and coordination with his accountant—a longtime friend and silent ally.

That morning's call gave David full access—unlocking Belize, the British Virgin Islands, and the quiet trust he'd built years earlier. Cassandra had no keys. No passwords. No leverage. Nothing linked to her shell company.

Her scaffolding was noise—temporary, hollow, designed to distract. His financial structure ran deeper. It wasn't decoration. It was foundation. Built to last.

Then David found something else.

Her credit card statements revealed another life—$47,000 spent over eight months. Curated. Concealed. Ultimately redirected into a private savings account with a beneficiary he didn't recognize. No banker. No lawyer. No connection. Just a name that led nowhere. A ghost.

Luxury lunches at Riverside Country Club. Spa treatments. Hermès handbags bought the same week she argued about grocery bills. Designer purchases timed to coincide with her "book club."

The receipts hadn't screamed. They'd waited—for clarity, for context, for confrontation.

Cassandra had taken sixteen months to rehearse her exit. David took three days to draft his defense. She underestimated the man who rose from poverty. A finance major. A builder. She catalogued the visible kingdom while the crown jewels lay hidden in plain sight.

She hadn't been managing the household. She'd been staging her escape.

And now, David was preparing his counterattack.

There would be audits. Depositions. He would pursue them to the fullest extent of the law. Cassandra and Juan hadn't just taken money—they had stolen years. Identity. Integrity. And David intended to reclaim every thread they tried to unravel.

He took inventory. Gathered proof. And made sure the reckoning came with receipts. He wasn't the kind of good man who kept turning the other cheek. He was the kind who made silence speak in court.

They should have known better.

He didn't belong to them. Not then. Not now.

He belonged to himself.

And this time, he wasn't just breathing.

He was unraveling the con.

CHAPTER 24

THE BLUEPRINT OF DECEPTION

David sat in a conference room with Detectives Ramirez and Mendez, forensic accountant Lisa Tran, and his attorney, Robert Klein. Manila folders, spreadsheets, and legal documents covered the table—his entire financial life laid bare under harsh fluorescent lights.

"How bad is it?" David asked, bracing for the confirmation he already knew.

Robert glanced at Lisa. "Bad. But hopefully not irreversible."

David leaned forward. "Is it confirmed? The six hundred?"

Lisa nodded, her tone clinical. "Yes. About six hundred thousand siphoned over eight months. The rest of your accounts appear untouched."

The confirmation landed like a blow—not because it was new, but because it was undeniable. Money he and Elena had spent years saving. Money meant to secure their future, fund scholarships, preserve their legacy.

Robert continued, "That's just the beginning. If Cassandra and Juan hadn't been stopped, they would've drained the remaining funds and moved on to the real estate."

Lisa added, "Your home is valued at approximately $750,000. Their next move was to take out a line of credit—up to 80% of the equity."

David exhaled. "How can someone just steal everything like that?"

Lisa didn't soften the truth. "The documentation is airtight. You signed over access. You moved personal assets into joint holdings. And because you did it voluntarily—believing you were protecting your shared future—the transfers may be considered lawful."

David exhaled slowly, the weight of it settling in his chest. "I handed her the blueprint," he said. "Every signature. Every shared password. Not out of carelessness—but belief."

He looked down, jaw tight but eyes clear. "She didn't just steal from me. She weaponized my trust."

Mendez leaned in. "She wasn't just a gold digger. And Juan wasn't just a con man. They're professional predators. They study men like you—successful, generous, emotionally available. They build trust, marry into your life, and dismantle it from the inside."

David looked at the table, then caught his reflection in the darkened window. The man staring back was the same humble man he'd always been—but something had shifted. The naïve, trusting man who had fallen in love with Cassandra was gone. In his place was someone harder. Sharper. Angrier.

"I wonder how many others there are," he said quietly.

"We don't know yet," Robert admitted. "But given the sophistication of the con, we suspect you weren't the first. And you definitely weren't going to be the last."

The illusion was gone. But the hunt had only begun.

Later that day, David joined Mendez and the task force in a briefing room lined with whiteboards and digital monitors. He studied the investigation board with professional focus. Cassandra sat at the center, surrounded by operational support.

Juan handled the technical side—digital footprints, online personas, financial transfers. Cassandra, the face of the operation, forged emotional connections and extracted personal information from conversations victims believed were intimate.

David's stomach tightened as he examined the behavioral profile. There were no formal complaints, no prosecutions—just patterns. Men who had come forward briefly, then disappeared from the process, too ashamed or protective of their reputations to press charges.

"Their targeting is strategic," the behavioral analyst explained. "Men with substantial assets and recent emotional loss. Vulnerability creates openings."

Her laptop revealed targeted social events—galas, mixers, finance-heavy happy hours—where she studied routines, vulnerabilities, and the subtle tells—the small, unconscious signs people give that reveal their true feelings or intentions.

She didn't improvise. She engineered.

At the center of the board sat David's profile, surrounded by anonymized composites—professionals in their forties and fifties, mostly widowers or recently divorced. The analyst noted Cassandra's emotional precision: companionship, admiration, security. It wasn't random. It was tailored.

"What's remarkable," the analyst added, "is how Cassandra adapts to each victim's emotional needs. Most people think they'd notice the signs. But predators like her don't wear masks. They arrive as tenderness, helpfulness, romance. Sometimes, ten years younger. David, what happened to you isn't rare. It's just rarely prosecuted."

The truth settled in David's chest—not as revelation, but as ruin. Cassandra hadn't just read him—she had reverse-engineered him. The loneliness after Elena's death. The craving for connection. The ache to feel needed. She mirrored his grief, echoed his hopes, and fed him the illusion of renewal.

She spoke of children, legacy, building something sacred. Left parenting books on the nightstand. Asked about nursery colors. Wrapped her manipulation in tenderness until David wasn't just trusting her—he was building a life around her.

Every vulnerability became a blueprint. And he followed it, hook, line, and sinker.

He absorbed the information with growing resolve. The complexity didn't intimidate him—it fueled his determination to dismantle it.

The audit widened—emails, phone logs, visits to Merrill Lynch. Screenshots showed Cassandra with financial adviser Michael Stevens. Retirement plans labeled Phase Two. She hadn't just studied David's future—she'd mapped it.

Then came the chill: email logs revealed a relationship both romantic and conspiratorial. Juan had drafted the blueprint—a final heist to fund their escape. The target: David's $1.2 million. Their golden parachute.

She and Juan designed a new life—funded by David's savings and built on the scaffolding of his generosity. It wasn't just theft. It was reinvention.

The most damning file: Withdrawal Schedule—a fifteen-month plan to drain David's accounts. Transfers timed to avoid suspicion. Expenses fabricated to justify withdrawals. "She treated robbing David like a business plan," the detective said.

Offshore accounts. Shell companies. Searches for countries without extradition treaties. What began as petty theft had metastasized into a full-scale criminal enterprise—structured, rehearsed, chillingly precise.

While she executed the plan, David kept building—never suspecting his trust was being weaponized.

The final meeting with forensic accountants felt less like closure, more like autopsy. David sat across from them in a sterile conference room, the fluorescent lights unforgiving. Their analysis was colder than grief, sharper than rage.

His account had dropped from $1.2 million to $602,000—not a single heist, but a slow bleed. Withdrawals disguised as expenses. Spa visits coded as wellness reimbursements. Luxury purchases as home improvements. Even charitable donations rerouted to dummy foundations.

But the numbers were only part of the story.

Recovered emails. Altered file details. Encrypted messages. Cassandra's psychological blueprint emerged—not a woman cornered by circumstance, but one sculpting control. Her gestures—joint planning, soft suggestions—weren't signs of intimacy. They were tools of manipulation.

Even Michael Stevens, David's longtime adviser, had unknowingly helped her. Thinking he was supporting thoughtful investments, he helped establish the shell company. When Mendez showed him the timeline, he collapsed into a chair. "She used my integrity," he whispered. "She weaponized my loyalty."

The lead accountant closed the file. "She didn't just steal," he said. "She reclassified theft as care."

David didn't respond. He didn't need to. The numbers had already spoken.

With the con exposed and documented, Mendez had what she needed. This wasn't deception—it was financial crime in motion: fraud, conspiracy, intent to flee.

Merrill Lynch launched its own audit. The broker who processed Cassandra's transfers was placed on review. But every authorization bore David's consent. No breach. No liability. The system hadn't failed—it had worked exactly as designed. Just not for the person it was meant to protect.

The findings were quietly filed. Michael resigned, citing "personal disillusionment." And David, left with the aftermath, began the slow work of disentangling memory from manipulation.

The consequences rippled outward—through institutions, reputations, relationships. Cassandra hadn't just stolen. She eroded trust, structure, and the quiet belief that care couldn't be weaponized.

A full-scale manhunt began. Warrants expedited. Border alerts issued. Cassandra wasn't just fleeing David—she was fleeing consequence.

The illusion was gone.

But the hunt was just beginning.

THE RECALIBRATION

They left David's house at 6:30 p.m. in two cars—Juan in his, Cassandra in hers. No goodbyes, no trace. Cassandra packed what she could in under ten minutes. Juan took the lead, and together they slipped into the evening traffic, headlights carving through the dusk.

The road stretched out ahead, but an invisible distance had already settled between them. Each sat alone in their own car, swallowed by a swirl of restless thoughts, the silence pressing in so heavily it was almost deafening. Words hovered on the edges of the air—unspoken, fragile—never quite bridging the space that separated them.

Just past the bridge, Juan flicked on his signal—a quiet, deliberate gesture. Cassandra understood. He veered toward the rest area, and she followed.

Beneath the hum of vending machines and the low buzz of fluorescent lights, they finally spoke.

Juan didn't waste time. "We should've gone straight to JFK."

Cassandra shook her head, breath still uneven. "They flagged the account. The moment David filed, customs would've been notified."

Juan's jaw tightened. "We could've driven south."

"To what?" she shot back. "Panama? Belize? You want to cross three borders with fake papers and a duffel bag of cash? We'd be stopped before Virginia."

He exhaled, frustrated. "So what now?"

Cassandra steadied herself. "We wait. We recalibrate."

There was little else to say. Just a lot to absorb. David's confrontation had left its mark—not in bruises or broken plans, but in the quiet reckoning that followed.

By nightfall, they were in Newark, tucked inside a third floor walk up Juan had kept under a cousin's name. The apartment was spare—linoleum floors, a full size bed, a rotary phone with no answering machine. Cassandra drew the curtains. Juan unplugged the TV.

They stayed inside for days.

The first week passed in silence. Cassandra monitored the news, but there was nothing—no names, no charges, no trace of David. Then came the ripple. A customer at a Midtown lounge mentioned a police investigation—quiet, federal, and serious. Said he had ties to the department. A man from Cold Spring was pressing charges. Fraud. Shell companies. Frozen accounts.

Cassandra didn't need headlines. That was enough. The final transfer hadn't cleared. The shell company—the legal entity she'd used to move money—had been locked down. No access. No escape.

Juan paced. "So we wait?"

"We recalibrate," she repeated.

She sat on the edge of the bed, staring at the duffel. Inside: bundled cash, a folder of cashier's checks—everything they'd managed to withdraw before the freeze. Roughly $200,000. Not enough to disappear forever, but enough to negotiate.

Then her breath caught. A beat. A tightening.

"Shit… the laptop."

Juan froze mid step. "Are you sure?"

"I left it in the study," she said, voice rising. "The one with the shell routing, the offshore logs, the alias spreadsheets. Everything."

Juan dragged both hands down his face. "That's the key. If they crack that, they'll trace the wires. They'll find the accounts."

Cassandra nodded slowly. "They'll find them, yes. But they can't touch them. Not directly. The banks are offshore—outside U.S. jurisdiction."

Juan paced harder. "Unless they get cooperation."

"They'd need the logs first. Then a treaty. Then a bank willing to play nice. That takes time."

Juan exhaled. "So we still have the money."

"For now," she said. "But if they move fast, and the bank folds under pressure…"

She didn't finish. She didn't need to.

Cassandra stared at the wall. "We didn't just leave a trail. We left the blueprint.

They waited three more weeks. Cassandra kept the blinds closed and the radio low.

No confirmed sightings. No surveillance hits. But she knew the net was tightening. Airports were no longer an option. The offshore accounts remained untouched—for now. But they couldn't stay in Newark forever.

Juan grew restless. He wanted motion. Cassandra wanted control.

She proposed a meeting with David—negotiation, not confrontation. On the kitchen table, she spread out a paper map of Manhattan and circled Bryant Park. Southeast corner. Near the carousel.

"This is where we'll meet him."

Juan frowned. "You think he'll show?"

"I think he wants answers," she said. "Not a trial. Not a chase. Just clarity. He needs to understand what happened."

Juan crossed his arms. "You're gambling."

"I'm calculating," she replied. "David doesn't pivot—he processes. If I control the tone—no lawyers, no police—he'll listen."

Juan glanced at the folder of cashier's checks. "That's all we've got left?"

"That's all we need," she said. "It's bait."

He sat down, rubbing his temples. "And if he doesn't bite?"

"Then we vanish," she said. "But we try this first."

She walked to the window, watching the pay phone blink across the street. "Tomorrow," she said. "I'll make the call. No trace. No callback. Just a time and a place."

Juan didn't respond. He didn't need to. The silence between them was no longer tense—it was tactical.

Outside, Newark moved without noticing them. Inside, the plan crystallized.

CHAPTER 26

THE BAIT

A month had passed since David uncovered the deception. Juan and Cassandra had vanished—no sightings, no transactions, no digital trace. They hadn't just evaded capture. They had evaporated.

David followed up weekly. Mendez never made promises.

"We're working on it," she said, voice clipped. "Interpol alerts are active. Border flags raised. No leads. For all we know, they've left the country."

But David knew better. They hadn't left. Not yet.

The silence was its own kind of violence. Cassandra hadn't just stolen money—she'd stolen momentum. The investigation had stalled. The reckoning was suspended. And David, once the plaintiff, now felt like a placeholder in his own case.

Some nights, he imagined them in transit—Juan driving, Cassandra watching the rearview mirror, her expression unreadable. A motel off-grid. A passport under a different name. A life rehearsed in whispers.

But his gut told him they hadn't gone far. He suspected they were still close—waiting, recalibrating.

Then, one evening, the phone rang.

He answered out of habit, not expectation.

"David."

Her voice was calm. Controlled. Not remorseful—just familiar enough to disarm.

"What do you want, Cassandra."

"To talk." A beat. "To negotiate."

David said nothing.

"Juan and I are leaving the country in a few days," she continued. "But travel isn't safe. Not with the Interpol alerts. And not with the laptop we left in your study."

David's jaw tightened. "The laptop."

"Yes," she said. "The one with the shell routing. The offshore logs. The alias spreadsheets. Everything. You know what's on it."

Still, he didn't speak.

"If you drop the charges," she said softly, "I'll return part of the money. No lawyers. No police. Just one conversation."

The silence stretched. Cassandra didn't fill it.

Finally:

"I'll meet you."

She exhaled—quiet, measured. "Bryant Park. Southeast corner, near the carousel."

The line went dead.

She'd called from a pay phone. No number. No trace. No way to call her back.

David stared at the receiver, then picked it up again and called Detective Mendez.

"She wants to meet," he said. "I agreed. Bryant Park. Public. She thinks I'll come alone."

Mendez didn't hesitate. "We'll be there. No confrontation. No tip-off. Just presence."

Up to that point, Cassandra and Juan had gone dark. No confirmed address. No flight records. No surveillance hits. The shell company was quiet. The $600,000 siphoned from David's accounts had vanished— likely split between offshore wires and cash withdrawals. They weren't just hiding. They were preparing to disappear.

"This could be our opening," Mendez said. "If she shows up, we move."

David nodded. He understood. The meeting wasn't about closure—it was containment.

"Why would she reach out, knowing I'd already gone to the authorities?" he asked.

Mendez had a theory. "Cassandra was confident. Too confident. She thought you were still vulnerable, still open to charm. That she could spin one last story—offer just enough restitution to buy her freedom."

If David dropped the charges, the Interpol alerts would dissolve, the border flags would lift, and she and Juan could leave the country without scrutiny. The duffel bag of cash wasn't bait for a con—it was leverage for escape.

Maybe she saw the meeting as a final performance. One last act before the curtain fell.

But it was a miscalculation.

Cassandra didn't realize how completely David had changed. His trust had hardened into resolve. She didn't see how deeply he despised her.

The thought of facing her again didn't soften him—it sharpened him. His anger, once tangled in confusion, had crystallized. And the complexity of the operation only fueled his determination to dismantle it. To take them down.

An old phrase flickered in his mind: a thin line between love and hate. He used to dismiss it as a cliché—something people said when they couldn't make sense of their feelings. But now, he understood. It wasn't a line. It was a gravitational shift.

One day, you're pulled in—drawn by something you can't resist. The next, you're pushed away, repelled with equal force.

It wasn't something you could grasp intellectually. You had to live it to know it.

Just weeks ago, he would have defended Cassandra against every warning, every doubt. He believed he was in love.

But today, he despised her—not just for what she'd done, but for how deliberately she'd done it.

This wasn't a lapse. It was design. Betrayal built brick by brick. Architectural in its cruelty. And that made it unforgivable.

That night, he sat in his study, surrounded by relics of foresight—retirement forecasts, immaculate ledgers, and a photo of Cassandra laughing. It no longer held warmth. Only proof of a well-constructed illusion.

Bryant Park had once been their place. Sunday coffees. Quiet walks. A bench near the carousel where she once told him she wanted children.

Now, it would be the stage for her undoing.

THE TAKEDOWN

David had rehearsed this moment in silence. In sleepless nights. In the quiet ache of realization. Now, it was here.

Cassandra arrived first, dressed in soft blue linen, her hair pulled back in a loose clip—serene, elegant, composed. She looked like someone who had never fled, never lied, never siphoned a life into offshore accounts. She chose the bench deliberately—the one near the carousel in Bryant Park, where she'd once told David she wanted children.

Juan lingered several paces behind, scanning the surroundings like a soldier wired for threat. His jaw was tight. His eyes moved constantly. He didn't trust the quiet. He didn't trust the plan. But he trusted her.

They had agreed in Newark: this was the only way. If David dropped the charges, the alerts would lift, the borders would open, and they could disappear cleanly. The duffel bag of cash was real. The offer was real. The risk was calculated.

They presented a united front. Cassandra had insisted. Juan had agreed—not reluctantly, but with the clarity of someone who understood the stakes. There was no margin for error. No second attempt. This was the recalibration—the pivot from hiding to escape.

Cassandra believed in her ability to recalibrate any room, any man. This wasn't nostalgia—it was strategy. David had loved her once. That was leverage. That was currency. She didn't need forgiveness. She needed clearance. She didn't come to explain. She came to negotiate.

David was already seated. Composed. Unmoving. He hadn't stood when she arrived. He hadn't flinched. He watched her the way a man watches a storm he's already survived—not with fear, but with clarity.

Cassandra smiled. Not warmly. Not falsely. Just enough to test the air. She still believed she could steer the moment.

She sat down and leaned in, voice low. "I can return some of the money. Not all. But enough to make this go away."

David nodded once. "I'm listening."

She eased the duffel onto the bench between them, unzipped it just enough to reveal the edge of bundled cash—neat stacks, rubber-banded, deliberate. Beneath them, a folder of cashier's checks. She didn't push it toward him. She let it sit. Visible. Tactile. Real.

"Two hundred thousand," she said. "Cash. No lawyers. No police. You drop the charges, and we walk away clean."

David didn't blink. He let the silence stretch. He was going to play along.

"If you want me to drop the charges," he said, "you'll have to do better than two hundred thousand."

"David, let me explain," she added quickly, ignoring the negotiation. "It got out of hand. I never meant—"

"To get caught?" David interrupted.

She flinched.

Juan slipped into a table nearby, close enough to hear but pointedly removed. He wasn't there to run. He was there to monitor. They'd agreed on this—every word, every risk. This was the recalibration.

David placed a manila folder on the table between them—spreadsheets, transfer receipts, digital timestamps. Every betrayal accounted for.

"I know," he said, steady. "Everything. So you see, Cassandra—your two hundred thousand won't do it for me."

He paused. "You siphoned nearly six hundred thousand. And now you're offering me a third of it, like you're doing me a favor."

Cassandra's fingers brushed the folder like it held memories instead of evidence. Her voice remained calm. "We were supposed to be gone. The last wire was scheduled for Friday. You came home Thursday."

David didn't flinch. "So I interrupted the exit."

She nodded, unapologetic.

He leaned in slightly, voice low but clear. "I've seen the offshore wires. The fees alone would've cost you tens of thousands. But even with that, you moved hundreds of thousands—into accounts I now have the routing for."

He tapped the folder. "The laptop has everything. Alias spreadsheets. Transfer logs. The blueprint. And the authorities have it now. You think this ends with your duffel bag? It doesn't. I'm going after all of it."

Juan spoke then, quiet but firm. "You can try. But those banks won't cooperate. Not with U.S. authorities. That money's buried. Even with the logs, they'll hit a wall."

Cassandra added, "We're not denying what we did. But you're chasing ghosts. The only money you'll ever see is in that bag."

David let the silence stretch. "You're not offering restitution. You're offering bait. Just enough to make me hesitate—just enough to buy your exit."

She didn't deny it.

He looked at her, unflinching. "This isn't generosity. It's survival. You're not trying to make it right. You're trying to make the legal problem go away."

Cassandra's mask cracked—just slightly.

"I didn't come here to beg, David. I came to negotiate. Survival isn't sentimental."

She paused, studying him. The offer had failed. The leverage had shifted. But Cassandra wasn't finished—she recalibrated.

"You need to step back and think about what you contributed to this," she said. "You designed the blueprint. I just walked the path you paved. You gave me access to everything. You were predictable. Kind. Trusting. I didn't destroy you."

The words didn't cut. They confirmed.

"You were an easy mark," she added, voice flat.

He blinked, stunned.

"And the children?" David asked. "The ones you said you wanted—the ones we planned for?"

"You wanted a family. I gave you the fantasy."

"You were taking birth control."

"I was never going to have your children, David. That was never part of the plan."

He stared at her, hollowed out.

"You used that to convince me," he said. "You said you needed security. That if something happened to me, you and the kids would need a place to live."

She nodded, unapologetic. "And you added me to the deed. Opened joint accounts. Rewrote your will. You gave me everything I needed."

"I thought I was building a life."

"You were," she said. "Just not yours."

Then she looked at him, eyes steady. "You were the easiest mark I've ever worked."

The word hit him like a slap.

Mark. Not partner. Not husband. Just a target. A job. A means to an end.

David leaned back, watching the final cracks splinter—not in the finances, but in the myth they'd built together. The con wasn't unraveling. It was combusting.

Cassandra leaned in again, voice low. "You didn't want truth—you wanted beauty. And I gave you illusion."

Juan spoke next, voice low and deliberate. "And the brother act? That was her idea. Said it would make the affair more thrilling. Can't believe you fell for that one."

David's breath caught, but he didn't look away.

Cassandra stood, voice slicing through the silence. "Do we have a deal?"

David didn't answer.

That was the cue.

From a weathered bench nearby, Detective Mendez stood. Two plainclothes officers emerged from opposite directions, their approach silent, their timing exact. They'd heard everything. The wire had done its job. David had guided the conversation—calm, deliberate, surgical. Cassandra and Juan had admitted to fraud, wire transfers, and deception. It was enough to convict.

The con hadn't unraveled. It had been dismantled.

Cassandra froze mid-step. Her eyes met David's—just for a moment. And in that flicker, something shifted. Not remorse. Not fear. Recognition. She'd been outplayed. The mark had become the architect.

Juan didn't move. His posture remained steady, his gaze unreadable. He wasn't surprised. He'd known the risks, rehearsed the fallout. This wasn't a miscalculation—it was contingency.

As the cuffs snapped around her wrists, Cassandra's smile fractured—sharp now, cruel. She didn't resist. She didn't speak. But her silence was venomous.

Juan stared hollowly, jaw clenched—not with grief, but calculation.

He spoke—just loud enough for Mendez to hear. "We set up joint access for emergencies. In case one of us was incapacitated. But she moved the funds. I'm willing to negotiate. I'll testify."

Mendez, knowing Cassandra was the face of the con—the wife, the one with the most to gain—wanted leverage. She nodded once. "Let's see what you can offer at the station."

Cassandra's head whipped toward him. "He's lying," she hissed.

Juan didn't flinch. "Detective, tell me what you need. I'll cooperate. I'll walk you through everything."

David didn't respond. He watched them fracture—not as lovers or allies, but as constructs shedding their masks in a bid for survival. But Juan wasn't fracturing. He was curating.

His voice steady. His posture measured. He didn't deflect—he redirected. Cassandra's collapse became his alibi. Her ambition, his shield. And David, still absorbing, hadn't yet seen the deeper con.

Juan wasn't claiming innocence. He was repositioning guilt. Every sentence, a pivot. Every glance, a rehearsal. He wasn't cooperating—he was auditioning for immunity.

Cassandra saw it. Her silence cracked into breathless fury. "You planned this," she spat.

Juan didn't deny it. He looked at Mendez. "I'm ready."

Cassandra turned to David, eyes sharp. "You think this is justice? You think he's clean?"

David stood slowly. "I don't think he's clean. But I think you deserve each other—no matter what comes next."

Mendez nodded. "We'll sort the rest in custody."

One officer collected the manila folder. Another took the duffel bag—cash, cashier's checks, all of it—tagged and sealed as evidence.

Juan didn't flinch. Cassandra didn't speak again.

As they were led away—separately, deliberately—David remained at the bench. The carousel spun behind him, soft music drifting through the park like a lullaby for ghosts.

He didn't feel vindicated. He felt emptied.

The illusion hadn't collapsed. It had calcified—into evidence, into silence, into a truth too sharp to mourn.

He looked down at the table. The folder was gone. But the betrayal remained—undocumented, unspoken.

David stood. The carousel turned. And the reckoning was complete.

The storm had passed. Not with thunder, but with revelation.

That night, David was spent. He hadn't realized how tightly he'd held himself—how long he'd been bracing for impact. Now, the adrenaline had drained, leaving behind a dull ache in his shoulders, his jaw, his hands. His body felt used, like armor that had outlasted the battle.

He returned to silence. Not the hollow kind, but the kind that listens—a silence that settled into walls, into untouched wine glasses, into routines that hadn't betrayed him, only waited.

The house felt different. Not just quieter—but lighter. The air no longer carried Cassandra's manipulation or Juan's calculation. The rooms, once tense with performance, had softened.

He sat in the living room, surrounded by the familiar. Nothing had changed, and yet everything had. The space felt returned to him, as if the walls had exhaled.

She had called him an easy mark. And maybe he was. Not because he was naïve, but because he was open. Because he believed in legacy, in devotion, in the quiet dignity of building a life.

Closure hadn't come through confrontation. It came through clarity.

Healing doesn't arrive with thunder. It creeps in—threading itself through reclaimed rituals: morning light on clean sheets, walks where no eyes followed, no heart lied.

Cassandra hadn't shattered him. She'd revealed the fracture lines he'd refused to see.

Love isn't always the antidote to illusion. Sometimes, it's its most elegant disguise.

And so, David Ortiz—scarred but sovereign—sat beneath a lamp's warm glow, in a house that finally felt like his again, and began the quiet, sacred work of turning the page.

PART III

THE RECKONING —
THE RECLAMATION

"Healing isn't loud. It's the sound of breath returning to a room."

CHAPTER 28

THE LIGHT STAYED ON

Three days after Bryant Park, David stood at the edge of his sister's driveway, hands in his pockets, dignity unraveling thread by thread.

He hadn't slept much since the arrest. The adrenaline had faded, but the reckoning hadn't. Cassandra was in custody. Juan was cooperating. The wire had done its job.

But now came the part David had postponed—not out of avoidance, but necessity. He couldn't face his family without resolution. Not while the storm was still circling.

They had warned him. Quietly. Kindly. They had seen through Cassandra's charm, asked questions he'd brushed aside. And now, he owed them the truth.

The porch light glowed softly above the door—steady, unblinking, as if it had been waiting for him. It didn't flicker. It didn't judge. It simply stayed on.

The wind pressed against his coat—not with urgency, but with the hush that precedes confession. He hadn't called ahead. Hadn't rehearsed what he'd say. He wasn't sure he was welcome.

But the light said otherwise.

And so he stepped forward.

Reina opened the door slowly, brows lifted in quiet surprise. She hadn't expected anyone—least of all her brother. Her gaze lingered, searching his face for context, for explanation.

He looked worn. Not broken, but stripped down. The man who once preached self-reliance and defended Cassandra like scripture now stood silent on her porch, humbled, hands in his pocket.

She didn't speak at first. The silence between them was thick—not hostile, but heavy with history.

"I burned it all," David said, voice low, carved from stone. "The trust. The warnings. I should've listened."

Reina's eyes narrowed—not in judgment, but in recognition. She didn't ask what happened. She didn't need to. Cassandra's absence said enough.

"So it's over," she said quietly. "Or close enough."

David nodded.

Reina stepped aside, motioning him in. "We'll talk. But first— let's eat."

After David set down his bag, Reina stepped into the hallway and made a few quiet calls. Within the hour, Teresa, Luz, and his parents arrived—no questions, no delay. These were the people closest to him, dropping everything to come to his aid, bearing wine, dessert, and cautious eyes.

No one asked why. They already knew.

The dining room was modest and warm: a worn oak table, mismatched chairs, a hand-stitched runner. The scent of lentils and roasted chicken hung in the air. It wasn't lavish, but it was theirs.

Despite arriving in this country with little more than grit and faith, the Ortiz siblings had done well. Each had worked hard, built lives, and owned their own homes. And though Reina wasn't the matriarch, she had been the first to make the leap—the one who navigated the paperwork, the housing, the jobs.

As the eldest sister, she had become their quiet anchor—the one they looked to when things got hard.

That's why David had come to her first. Not for absolution. For ground.

They ate together, the table full but quiet. Forks clinked. Porcelain scraped. The air held a kind of reverence—no judgment, just waiting.

Reina's teenage daughter, Sandra, lingered in the doorway. She had adored Elena once. Now she looked at David as if he belonged more to that memory than to this moment.

Her voice slipped gently into the quiet. "Did you forget about her?"

David lowered his fork. "No," he said. "I never forgot her. I just... tried to replace the pain she left behind. Not with love. Not with someone better. Just with something that made it hurt less."

Sandra didn't respond, but something in her gaze softened—like she finally understood the difference.

After dinner, the family moved to the backyard fire pit, wrapped in throw blankets, dusk settling like ash around them.

David sat with a chipped mug in his hands, steam rising like breath he hadn't yet taken. His body ached—from tension, restraint, and the weight of finally speaking the truth.

He spoke slowly, deliberately. No repetition. No dramatics. Just facts.

He explained what Cassandra had done: the siphoned accounts, the shell company, the chilling silence she left behind. He talked like a man building a case—as if betrayal demanded footnotes.

A ripple moved through the circle—anger, disbelief, something protective rising all at once.

Julio's jaw tightened. "Eso no fue un error, David. Eso fue un crimen."

Reina exhaled sharply. "She stole in your name. That kind of fraud follows a man."

Carmen shook her head, eyes soft but wounded. "Te puso en peligro, mijo. Legal y personal."

Then the family fell quiet again—absorbing the weight of what he'd endured. No one asked for more. They had heard enough.

David took a deep breath and looked around the circle, the fire casting flickers across their faces. He hadn't expected comfort. He'd braced for judgment. But what he found was something quieter—recognition. Their understanding settled around him like a permission he hadn't known he needed.

That recognition gave him the courage to go further, to speak the part he had kept buried—the part that had nothing to do with bank accounts or shell companies. The financial betrayal was one thing. What came next lived in a different category entirely.

David hesitated, his gaze dropping to the fire. "The theft wasn't the worst part," he said quietly. "What broke me wasn't the money—it was how they made a fool of me in my own house."

The words seemed to cost him something, but he pushed on, determined to give his family the truth they deserved.

He told them how he had walked in and found Cassandra and Juan together. Not siblings. Not family. Lovers. Partners in the con. The intimacy of it had struck harder than the fraud itself, a wound aimed at his pride as much as his heart.

In their culture, in their world, many men would have exploded. Many would have killed. But he had walked out instead—shaking, gutted, choosing restraint over rage, choosing truth over the kind of violence that ruins lives.

A heavy silence followed—one filled not with shock, but with the weight of understanding.

Teresa broke it first. Her voice carried the edge of someone who'd been burned and learned to name the flame.

"I've been waiting for this conversation," she said. "But I'm not here to gloat. I've been on the other side of heartbreak too. And I want you to hear something—even if it stings."

David looked up, eyes tired but open.

"Everybody plays the fool," she said. "Doesn't matter how smart you are, how careful. Love finds your blind spot—especially when someone hums your favorite song while you're aching for music."

She paused. "The mistake isn't wanting it—it's pretending it's safe."

"She lied to me," David said, voice low. "And I handed her every key without question."

Teresa's gaze softened. "Falling in love is easy," she said. "Seeing who you're loving—that's the hard part."

David closed his eyes.

"You saw second chances," she continued. "Laughter. Heaven on earth. She sold you the soundtrack. But you never saw who was holding the mic."

She leaned in, voice steady.

"You're not stupid. You're not weak. You're human. And heartbreak doesn't mean you failed—it means you felt something worth betting on."

David said nothing. The silence settled like grace.

"And yeah," Teresa added, "she used your heart like a tool. But that heart? It's still yours. You decide what happens next—not her."

Reina, the eldest, had been quiet until now. Her voice was calm but carried authority—the kind that comes from watching over all of them for years.

"She studied you," Reina said. "Not just your habits—your hopes. That's what makes it cruel. She didn't just take money. She took your rhythm."

She looked at David carefully. "But you're here. You're speaking. That means she didn't take your voice."

Julio, their father, sat with his hands folded over his knees. When he finally spoke, his voice was low, deliberate—like someone who didn't waste words.

"You were raised to trust," he said. "To believe in the good. That's not weakness, David. That's legacy."

Carmen, their mother, reached for David's hand. Her grip was gentle but firm—like the hands that had once cared for him and bandaged his knees.

"We taught you to build," she said. "To love with your whole heart. We didn't teach you how to spot a thief wearing kindness. That's not your fault."

Luz, the youngest sister, leaned in, voice soft but clear—always the quiet observer, now stepping forward.

"You didn't see what we saw," she said. "But now you do. That's what matters."

David nodded slowly. "I didn't see it," he admitted. "Not then. I saw what I needed to see—what I wanted to believe. But my eyes are wide open now."

Reina's voice softened. "Good," she said. "That's the David I remember."

Luz leaned in, her voice steady. "You didn't let rage write the ending. That matters."

Julio shifted forward, his tone firm but full of pride. "You may have lost money, but you didn't lose yourself. Your mother and I are proud of how you handled it—with restraint, with dignity. That kind of betrayal could've pulled anyone into violence. But you didn't let it."

He paused, letting the truth settle. "Had you acted on that rage, you'd have buried the truth in blood. You would've erased the betrayal with vengeance—and made them the victims. We'd be having a very different conversation right now. You can replace money and material things, but your self-respect, your peace of mind, and your freedom are priceless."

Only then—after the emotional truth had been spoken and held—did David straighten, his voice gaining clarity.

"I'm not just reacting," he said. "I'm taking action. I've already spoken to the detectives. I'll pursue charges against both Cassandra and Juan—to the fullest extent of the law."

No one interrupted. No one questioned his resolve. Instead, heads nodded slowly, one after another. There was quiet consensus around the fire: this was the right path. Not vengeance. Not spectacle. Just truth, pursued with clarity.

David exhaled—long, deliberate. The ache was still there, but it had shape now. Direction.

"I'm done being the mark," he said. "Now I'm the witness."

The weekend with his family had been long—heavy with truth, threaded with restoration. Difficult conversations with no simple resolutions. But there was presence. There was listening. And in that quiet labor of love, something in David began to realign.

That night, he sat with a glass of wine. The house was quiet—but not empty. Something had been stripped from him, yes. But something else had returned: rhythm, clarity, and resolve.

The ache hadn't vanished. It had simply found direction.

He didn't reach for distraction. He didn't revisit the past. Instead, he chose to begin again—not with denial, not with bravado, but with intention. To rebuild. To flourish.

Outside Reina's house, the porch light stayed on—steady, unblinking. A silent witness. A signal that the pieces were his to gather.

Inside, David Ortiz—weathered but unwavering—began again. Not with vengeance. Not with illusion. But with truth, and the quiet strength of knowing he would never be the mark again.

CHAPTER 29

WHAT WE CHOOSE TO SEE

The following weekend, David had dinner with Junior. Afterward, they sat in the garage, which still smelled of motor oil and old pine. Overhead, a single bulb swung gently, casting soft light across the cluttered workbench—socket wrenches, a faded Yankees cap, a bottle of rum half-wrapped in brown paper.

David poured rum into two paper cups. Junior leaned against a shelf stacked with old radio parts, his boot tapping a slow rhythm against the concrete.

"She asked me to add her to my accounts," David said, handing him a cup. "The house. Retirement. Everything. Said it was time. That if we were going to have kids, we needed to build like partners." He exhaled. "She made me feel alive again."

He chuckled, gaze low. "You think I was naïve?"

Junior paused mid-sip. "No. I think you were hopeful—holding on to the idea of a family. Naïve is not knowing better. Hope is seeing the risk and still stepping forward. That's what you did, hermano. And that leaves a deeper bruise."

Outside, the wind whispered and stirred, rising and falling like a warning.

"You never liked her," David said.

Junior shrugged. "No. But it wasn't just me. I trusted Marisol's read—her bullshit meter never fails. Said Cassandra wore charm like armor. That was enough."

David stared at the workbench. "What if I just needed her to be who I wanted?"

Junior set down his cup. "We all want something. Doesn't mean the wanting makes it real."

They sat in silence, the bulb swaying like a slow pendulum.

Junior leaned forward. "You didn't fail, David. You just loved someone who knew how to weaponize it. That's not on you."

David nodded, the ache in his chest loosening slightly.

"I'm pressing charges," he said. "Both of them. I'm done letting silence protect the wrong people."

Junior raised his cup. "Then here's to the truth. And to never mistaking charm for character again."

They clinked paper cups. The rum burned, but it steadied him—like truth swallowed in small doses.

The next morning, David woke with the kind of ache that wasn't physical—but cellular. It lived beneath the ribs, behind old laughter, in the corners where memory refused to dust itself off.

Luz had asked him to stop by her salon. She'd said it gently, almost offhand—"Come by tomorrow. Not for a haircut. For something quieter." The salon doubled as a wellness studio, a space she'd built with intention: part refuge, part ritual.

He dressed slowly. Drove across town. Hands steady. Mind replaying Cassandra's final words like a needle stuck on vinyl.

By the time he arrived, the sky had settled into a soft gray. Sage and amber tones glowed from within. Incense curled around potted plants and framed blessings. It was the kind of place that invited silence to speak.

The door closed softly behind him. David didn't speak. He didn't pace or clench his fists. He just stood there, shoulders low, eyes unfocused—like someone trying to hold still in a storm.

Luz met him with a calm nod and no questions. She poured chamomile tea into a stone cup and handed it to him.

"I keep telling myself I'm angry," he said, voice low. "Angry I didn't see the red flags. The façade."

"You're not angry," she said gently, her eyes steady. "You're heartbroken. Those are different ghosts."

David gripped the cup, warm against his palms, but didn't drink. "I feel like a fool. I saw a future... and she saw a bank account."

Luz stepped closer, her voice a thread in the quiet room. "You're not a fool, David. Cassandra was good at what she did. She knew exactly how to make a man feel chosen, and she used that talent on you."

Without a word, Luz walked to a chest near the altar. She unlocked it with care and returned with a box. Inside: a soft scarf, a letter, and a single dried flower—pressed and fragile.

"She left these here for you," Luz said quietly. "Tucked them away with no instructions. Just para después. Her words, not mine."

David's throat tightened. He hadn't cried in years, but something inside him buckled—Elena, even in death, had known he would need this moment.

"I asked her once what that meant," Luz continued. "She said I'd know when the time was right. I didn't—until now. After everything that's happened... the betrayal, the unraveling. You don't need answers, David. You need her voice. Her love. Something to hold onto that wasn't taken from you."

"She wore the scarf the day you danced under the ferry lights," Luz said. "Said it carried warmth. And the letter—she wrote that after the doctor gave her the news. She didn't want you to find her pain. She wanted you to find her love."

David reached in slowly. Touched the hibiscus—same kind Elena once tucked behind her ear on their honeymoon.

He unfolded the letter. Her handwriting curved across the page like sunlight.

Mi Amor,

You brought steadiness to my wild. And that's all I ever needed.

You were my best friend, my confidant, the love of my life.

I will always be by your side.

If the world ever makes you doubt yourself, remember this:

I saw your heart clearly. I saw your goodness. I saw the man you are.

I will always be by your side.

Siempre tuya, Elena

David read the words once, then again, as if they might shift under the weight of his grief. You brought steadiness to my wild. The line caught in his chest. It was Elena's voice—clear, unflinching, full of grace.

He felt the ache rise, not sharp but deep, like something long buried surfacing in the quiet. Her love had never asked him to prove himself. It had never twisted or withheld. It had simply been—constant, generous, true.

And now, in the aftermath of betrayal, when everything felt unmoored, her words steadied him again. Not with answers, but with remembrance.

Cassandra had left him questioning his worth. Elena reminded him he had once been someone's peace.

He pressed the letter to his chest, eyes closed. For the first time in weeks, the silence didn't feel empty—it felt sacred.

The tears came slowly—less a flood than a release.

Luz didn't speak. She placed a hand on his shoulder and closed her eyes.

And in the hush, the ache softened—not vanished, but changed. Like something quietly passing from memory into meaning.

David had agreed to meet Marisol at the café for old times' sake—to remember the days when she was the courier and confidant between him and Elena. Back then, she'd passed notes, guarded secrets, and held space for the kind of love that needed gentleness to grow.

By mid-afternoon, the café was nearly empty, sunlight spilling through the windows in slow, golden bands. David sat across from her, their coffee growing lukewarm between them. The hum of the espresso machine in the background was familiar—like the rhythm of memory gently revisiting itself.

"I keep thinking maybe I wanted Cassandra to be Elena," David admitted. "Not in how she looked. But in how she made the world feel less sharp."

Marisol didn't flinch. "Elena didn't protect you from pain, David. She helped you face it. She didn't soften the edges—she walked beside you through them."

He nodded slowly. "And Cassandra just made me want to pretend those feelings didn't exist."

"Cassandra wasn't a true partner," Marisol said gently. "She was a mirror for your illusions—for your longing to believe in a second once-in-a-lifetime kind of love. You found comfort in her, but it was built on projection."

She paused, thoughtful. "Elena stayed, even when things were hard. Even when you faltered. You were never a transaction to her. But Cassandra... she saw what was missing in your life. You wanted love. You wanted a family. So she reflected that fantasy—just enough to feel like truth."

David looked down. "Did you ever think I was blind?"

"No," Marisol said softly. "I thought you were reaching for something beautiful. A new beginning. The possibility of a family. Cassandra saw that. And she offered a promise she never intended to keep."

She paused again, her voice steady. "Cassandra wasn't just a lover. She became a symbol—of renewal, of what might come after loss. So when she betrayed you, it didn't just hurt in the present. It shattered the future you thought you were building."

Marisol leaned in slightly. "From where I stand, you're not just mourning her betrayal. You're mourning the hope she embodied—the version of yourself you believed you were becoming."

They sat together in a quiet that didn't ask for words—only presence. A silence that let truth settle without needing to be solved.

Outside, the light shifted across the sidewalk. Inside, David allowed the silence to name what he hadn't yet dared to speak aloud.

The ache hadn't vanished, but it no longer lived in secret. He had shared everything—every fracture, every truth. In doing so, he'd reclaimed something more than resolve. He'd reclaimed genuine connection with his friends and family.

As the next chapter loomed—courtrooms, filings, the slow machinery of justice—David felt ready. Not because the burden had disappeared, but because he no longer carried it alone.

That evening, David stared into his teacup, the steam rising as if it carried more than heat. The meeting with his family and friends had left him with much to consider. He thought about the warnings— Marisol's glances, Junior's hesitant pauses, his mother's weighted silences, Reina's quiet insistence. They had all seen it. They had all tried to say it. And he hadn't wanted to listen.

He asked himself:

Why is it that those closest to us see the truth first?

Why do they sense the fracture before it breaks?

Is it because they're not blinded by longing?

Or because they're not busy rewriting reality into what they need it to be? He didn't know the answer.

But now—two years later—he could still hear their voices. Not angry. Not dramatic. Just clear. The kind of clarity that comes only from love without agenda.

David hadn't been blind. He'd been selective. He saw what he needed to see to survive the emptiness. And in that moment, Cassandra wasn't a person—she was a possibility. A promise that love could return. That loneliness could be rewritten.

But love isn't a mask. And gut feelings aren't always loud. Intuition doesn't shout. It waits—quietly—in the eyes of those who know us better than we know ourselves.

Reina had once told him, "You're seeing what you want to see. But some of us see what's underneath the façade."

She was right. David hadn't been blind. He had been unwilling—because Cassandra had stepped into a space he was desperate to fill. She gave him what he thought he needed, and he clung to the illusion.

He didn't see heaven on earth; he needed it to be heaven, so he chose to believe it was.

CHAPTER 30

DUE PROCESS

The coverage arrived before the arraignment—brief, local, and speculative. A small column in The Cold Spring Ledger outlined the charges: Cassandra Jimenez, former real estate agent and wife of David Ortiz, taken into custody for financial fraud, wire transfers linked to offshore accounts, and aggravated deception.

David didn't respond publicly. He read just enough to confirm the facts hadn't been twisted. The rest, he let go. The truth was quieter than the noise. It didn't need headlines. It didn't seek attention. It simply waited—steady, unflinching, ready to be heard.

Cassandra faced multiple felony counts. Juan, though not initially indicted, was subpoenaed and questioned under oath. His immunity was conditional—fragile. The DA wanted a full picture. The case took shape not just from documents, but from patterns: the withdrawals, the false accounts, the months of manipulation dressed as love.

David gave a statement—recorded, sealed, and admissible.

Weeks passed. During that time, David sat down for a quiet interview with an independent journalist who specialized in stories of betrayal. She understood something most didn't: surviving deception wasn't about vindication. It was about reclaiming the self—rising beyond the shadows cast by manipulation and betrayal.

While others read brief articles in The Cold Spring Ledger, David lived the aftermath. He moved through his home with quiet purpose, purging what no longer belonged—not just objects, but the residue of her presence.

Each act was deliberate—a quiet purge of the energy she left behind, a way to make space for truth where illusion had once lived.

The arraignment was quiet, procedural. No cameras. No spectacle. Just the slow machinery of justice beginning to turn.

Cassandra stood before the judge in a crisp beige jumpsuit, wrists cuffed, expression unreadable. Her attorney, Lester Vaughn, entered with theatrical precision—sleek suit, cufflinks gleaming, voice calibrated for charm.

"Your Honor," he said, with a practiced nod, "my client pleads not guilty to all charges."

David sat in the gallery, unmoving. His expression was carved from stone. Beside him, his attorney, Lillian Cortez, took notes with surgical focus. The charges were read aloud—wire fraud, identity theft, conspiracy to defraud. Each one landed like a drumbeat.

The judge denied bail. The prosecution had argued successfully that Cassandra and Juan were flight risks, citing offshore accounts, falsified documents, and the scope of the deception. Vaughn objected, but the ruling stood.

From that point forward, the case entered its slow grind: filings, motions, depositions, forensic audits. A series of pretrial hearings followed—each one focused on admissibility of evidence, asset freezes, and the scope of discovery. With every session, another layer of the con was exposed.

Cassandra and Juan remained behind bars. Their faces faded from public view, but their presence lingered—in documents, in damages, in the cautious way David's financial advisor now spoke his name.

At a pretrial hearing focused on asset division, Vaughn addressed the bench with his signature flair.

"Under state law," he said, straightening his cuffs like punctuation, "Cassandra Jimenez is legally entitled to half of Mr. Ortiz's assets. She is his wife. And that makes her his partner—in love and in liability."

Lillian didn't flinch. "She wasn't a partner," she said, voice measured but firm. "She was a fraud. And fraud nullifies entitlement."

The judge didn't rule on Vaughn's motion that day. Instead, he scheduled additional hearings to review the claim and examine the evidence Lillian had submitted—bank records, shell company filings, and the wiretap transcripts that had triggered the investigation.

Eventually, the court set a trial date. The months leading up to it felt like paper cuts—thin, constant, and intimate. Reminders that the con hadn't ended with Cassandra's arrest. It had simply shifted stages.

After pleading not guilty, Cassandra gave performative interviews to sympathetic outlets, speaking of "emotional manipulation," painting herself as the misunderstood wife—controlled, isolated, victimized.

Juan remained silent. His deal was inked and sealed: full testimony in exchange for leniency.

It took nearly fourteen months for the case to reach the courtroom— months of filings, motions, and forensic audits that mapped the blueprint of the deception. The complexity of the fraud, the conditional immunity agreements, and the sheer volume of evidence demanded time. Justice moved slowly—but deliberately.

When the trial finally opened, the courtroom was hushed, expectant.

Prosecution's Opening Statement:

"Ladies and gentlemen of the jury, this case is not simply about financial misconduct—it is about betrayal cloaked in intimacy. The defendant, Cassandra Ortiz, entered into marriage not for love, but for leverage.

We will present evidence that shows her intent was fraudulent from the start: a calculated effort to gain access to David Ortiz's assets, routines, and vulnerabilities. This was not a partnership—it was a blueprint for exploitation.

Cassandra had no rightful claim to what she took. Her access was not earned through trust but engineered through deception. The law does not protect manipulation disguised as marriage. And today, we ask you to see through the performance and hold her accountable."

Defense's Opening Statement:

"Your honor, members of the jury, we urge you to remember that marriage is not a transaction—it is a union built on shared lives and mutual trust.

Cassandra Ortiz was not an outsider hacking into accounts or forging documents. She was David Ortiz's wife. She was given access, given authority, and acted within the bounds of that trust.

The prosecution will try to paint this marriage as a scheme. But we ask you to look at the facts: the shared accounts, the signed authorizations, the months of mutual decision-making.

This is not a case of theft—it is a case of broken trust between spouses. And broken trust, while painful, is not a crime."

The prosecution began with its strongest witness.

David took the stand with quiet precision—no pity sought, no rage offered. Just facts. Patterns of financial abuse. Juan's false identity. Handwritten ledgers. Bank statements. Phone records. He recounted the afternoon he came home unexpectedly and found them together—not with theatrics, but with clinical steadiness. No embellishment. Just sequence and detail.

During his testimony, the prosecution introduced the 911 recordings—captured during David's confrontation in his home—in which Cassandra and Juan confessed. They also played the Bryant Park recordings, where Cassandra admitted to the theft and offered David $200,000 to drop the case. The defense objected, citing admissibility concerns, but the judge ruled both recordings could be entered into evidence.

District Attorney Evelyn Grant led the prosecution, building her case on the meticulous work of Detective Mendez: months of cross-referencing financial records, interviewing witnesses, and reconstructing Cassandra's digital and paper trail with surgical precision. Grant's team cut clean through the final layer.

They demonstrated that Cassandra had forged David's signature on multiple legal documents, coordinated Juan's travel using handwritten itineraries, and outlined a multi-phase exit strategy in notes recovered from her laptop.

When the prosecution concluded its direct examination, the defense began its cross.

Vaughn approached the podium with measured calm, his tone deliberate but restrained. His strategy was clear: to reframe Cassandra's actions within the bounds of marital trust and shared authority—an effort to blur the line between betrayal and consent.

"Mr. Ortiz, did you give your wife, Cassandra Jimenez, full access to your accounts?"

"Yes."

"You also gave her full authority to manage those accounts?"

"Yes."

"Were there any written agreements outlining how she could or could not use those funds?"

"No."

"Did you ever question her financial decisions before discovering the alleged fraud?"

"No."

"Would you say you trusted her completely at the time?"

"Yes."

"Is it possible that some of the transactions you now view as deceptive were, at the time, consistent with her role as your spouse and financial partner?"

"Yes."

Vaughn paused, then nodded. "I have no further questions of this witness."

David stepped down from the stand and returned to his seat beside his attorney, Lillian Cortez—jaw set, eyes forward. Cassandra remained composed, but her stillness had shifted. No longer calculated. Now cornered.

The following day, Juan took the stand.

He wore a pressed suit, but his posture was rigid, his tone clinical. He didn't look at Cassandra. He didn't look at David. He looked past them—like someone presenting a case file, not recounting a betrayal.

He placed the blame squarely on Cassandra. She was the architect, the executor, the face of the plan. Juan described her as meticulous, persuasive, emotionally detached. She had selected David deliberately— after weeks of research, observation, and psychological profiling. She called him "the perfect mark."

With chilling precision, Juan laid out the blueprint of the long con: the timing of the relationship, the staged vulnerability, the financial entanglements, the forged documents. His testimony was surgical, devoid of emotion. The nail in Cassandra's coffin. Like someone reciting schematics—not remorse.

David didn't flinch. He absorbed each detail as the truth unraveled— quiet, deliberate, unshaken. When DA Grant asked why he went along with it, Juan answered flatly: "I believed in her. Until I didn't."

The courtroom remained silent. No gasps. No interruptions. Just the sound of Cassandra's myth collapsing under the weight of her own design. The jury watched her unravel in real time.

After Juan's direct testimony, the defense requested a sidebar. They did not cross-examine him. Faced with overwhelming evidence, they had seen the writing on the wall.

Canceled checks. Forged documents. Expert testimony. Juan's damning account. David's direct statements. The 911 recordings. The Bryant Park confession. The case had been built with precision—and it held.

Cassandra faced multiple felony counts. If sentenced consecutively, she risked more than twenty years in prison.

Vaughn advised Cassandra to change her plea and pursue a deal. She pleaded guilty to financial fraud, identity manipulation, and conspiracy to commit theft.

District Attorney Grant accepted the plea and negotiated an agreement capping her sentence at ten years, with eligibility for parole after six.

That same afternoon, the District Attorney and the defendant informed the judge of the changed plea. The judge accepted the plea deal and addressed the jury:

"Ladies and gentlemen of the jury, the parties have reached an agreement that resolves the charges without proceeding to trial. The District Attorney and the defendant have negotiated a plea deal, which this court has accepted. As a result, the defendant has entered guilty pleas to certain charges, and the court will now dismiss the jury. Your service is no longer required. Thank you for your attention and dedication throughout this process."

With that, the jury was excused, and the court proceeded with sentencing the following morning.

During the official sentencing, David gave his victim impact statement.

"They saw me as a dollar sign," he said, eyes fixed on Cassandra. "Not a human being. Just money walking around."

He spoke without theatrics, but each word landed with weight. He described how she had manipulated him from the beginning—researched him before they met, pretended to share his interests, mirrored his values.

"She was everything I thought I wanted," he said. "Kind. Spiritual. Interested in me as a person. She made me feel young again. But it was all an act."

"She was studying me. Learning my weaknesses. Figuring out how to get my money."

He paused, letting silence stretch across the room like a held breath.

"When I realized that every kiss, every 'I love you,' every moment of intimacy we shared was a lie—it was already too late. She never loved me. She was just waiting for the right moment to make her move."

His voice didn't rise. It didn't need to. The devastation was in the restraint.

"This betrayal didn't just take my money—it rewired me. I flinch at kindness now. I second-guess sincerity. I mistake warmth for strategy. That's what she stole. Not just trust. My ability to believe."

He looked down briefly, then back at the judge.

"I've spent countless nights trying to make sense of it. Trying to rebuild myself from the inside out. But this isn't about revenge. It's about naming what happened. It's about truth."

The courtroom was silent—not just still, but suspended. The air itself felt heavy. Some spectators sat motionless; others lowered their eyes, while a few watched Cassandra as if seeing her for the first time. A clerk stopped typing. A bailiff shifted, then stilled again.

The judge delivered the sentence.

Cassandra was sentenced to ten years, with eligibility for parole after six.

Juan received three years, credited with time served, meaning he would be released in one year.

David didn't look at her again. He had said what needed saying. And in that moment, something shifted—not erased, but released.

CHAPTER 31

PREPARING FOR THE NEXT CON

Cassandra didn't grieve the exposure—the courtroom, the headlines, the unraveling of her persona. Regret was for amateurs. What unsettled her was the stillness—the flatline of consequence. No audience. No improvisation. No leverage. Just time, stacked and sterile.

Concrete surrounded her like a judgment without voice. No mirror. No calendar. No color. Just a bunk, a shelf, and silence.

She rarely slept. Dreams arrived unscripted—improvisations with teeth. Her subconscious staged memories she couldn't curate: the persona she had crafted, and the woman who haunted it.

She hadn't written to Juan. Not out of anger, but irrelevance. He'd served his purpose. So had David. So had the system.

Everyone had played their part. From each, she'd extracted a lesson—how far charm could stretch, how quickly loyalty collapsed, how spectacle always outpaced nuance in the eyes of the law.

Her guilty plea wasn't confession. It wasn't remorse. It was clearance. A recalibration. The first move in a longer game.

The evidence had fenced her in. The performance was spent. And survival demanded a pivot.

Regret might visit. Remorse might flicker. But Cassandra wasn't built to linger. She was built to return.

What remained wasn't guilt—it was vacancy. The hollow left behind when manipulation loses its audience.

She missed the con, not the freedom. The con had rhythm, purpose, and a pulse. It was performance with stakes. Identity with teeth.

Behind bars, she felt the same way she had with David—trapped in a role she didn't believe, playing housewife to a man who mistook proximity for intimacy. That life had been its own kind of prison. This one just came with fewer props.

She didn't mourn the collapse. She studied it.

She hadn't misjudged David's intelligence—she'd misjudged his emotional depth. He'd been too close, too entangled. She'd mistaken calm for blindness. That was her error.

Next time, she wouldn't walk away empty-handed.

David had cost her more than she expected—not just in exposure, but in outcome. She'd underestimated the emotional architecture of the mark. She'd misread the depth, the durability. She'd left with nothing because she'd played the wrong game.

Next time, she'd build it differently. No entanglements. No improvisation. Just extraction. Clean and complete.

She didn't unravel. She recalibrated.

She needed to reinvent herself. It wouldn't happen quickly—but it would happen.

Trust had a long runway. What she lost in time, she gained in observation.

Even in prison, she studied people—how they folded into hierarchies, how they traded stories, how they forgot to guard their weaknesses. There was always a flaw. Always an angle.

She would be older when she got out. That much was certain.

Prison didn't just take time—it took currency.

She remembered what Juan once told her, half-drunk and half-serious: "Men want trophies, Cass. Not relics."

Beauty fades. Novelty expires. And the kind of men she used to manipulate would be chasing younger illusions by the time she saw daylight again.

Evolution was inevitable.

She would no longer be the face of the con—she'd become its architect. The strategist. The director.

She'd recruit younger, hungrier women to play the roles she once inhabited. She'd teach them how to walk the line between seduction and control, how to read a mark, how to vanish before the truth caught up.

She'd build the blueprint. They'd run the play.

She would use the years to refine her craft—new scripts, new tells, new exits. Even here, behind bars, there were stories to study, weaknesses to map, hierarchies to exploit.

The lessons from David and Juan weren't sentimental—they were structural.

She now understood how proximity distorts perception, how emotion clouds control, how exposure isn't failure—it's feedback.

She wouldn't emerge the same. She'd emerge better.

The con was what she knew best.

Six states away, Juan stood outside a halfway house with a paper folder and a borrowed identity.

His new name was Luis Vega—chosen for how easily it could disappear.

He'd shaved his beard. Wore slacks too long for his frame. The résumé was fabricated but plausible: warehouse assistant, inventory detail, quiet hours.

At intake, a woman with a clipboard asked, "Ever convicted?" He hesitated. Then lied.

She handed him a key. "Third floor. One week to prove you're useful."

Upstairs, he unpacked slowly, folding clothes with a reverence he hadn't earned. He aligned his toothbrush parallel to the sink.

That night, beneath a cracked ceiling, he counted silence instead of sleep. Before his eyes closed, he whispered to no one: "Never trust elegance when it arrives too early."

It wasn't an apology. It was a revision.

Juan complied. He showed up on time. Took inventory. Kept his head down.

The system expected obedience, so he gave it just enough. Probation had rules. He followed them. For now.

But beneath the surface, he watched.

The halfway house was a study in vulnerability—men trading stories too freely, staff revealing routines, systems built on trust and repetition.

Juan catalogued everything: who left doors unlocked, who forgot to log deliveries, who believed in redemption. He didn't miss Cassandra. He missed the game—the planning, the thrill of designing something invisible and precise.

She had been the face. He had been the spine. Now, he was learning to wear both.

The offshore money was still there—dormant, untouched.

Though the accounts were joint, he'd be released first. He would access it before she could.

It wasn't greed. It was insurance. A quiet reward for seeing the end before it arrived.

He couldn't touch it yet—not without triggering scrutiny. But it waited, like he did.

He didn't know if she'd come for it. She might. Cassandra didn't forget numbers. She didn't forget promises. If she came, it wouldn't be with rage. It would be with precision.

She didn't chase ghosts. She hunted leverage.

Cassandra had taught him how to vanish, how to build trust without truth. But she never taught him how to stay. And he never asked.

Most days, he wanted to forget she existed. But forgetting wasn't possible.

She hadn't ruined him. She had revealed him.

And that, he knew, was the deepest con of all.

He didn't know when he'd move again. But he would. Not with noise. Not with charm. With silence. With structure.

They weren't seeking redemption. They were adapting—quietly, deliberately. Separate paths, same instinct.

The collapse hadn't broken them; it had clarified them. The comeback wouldn't be loud or rushed. It would be patient, methodical, inevitable. They weren't just surviving. They were rehearsing. Refining. Preparing the next con in silence..

CHAPTER 32

REFUSING TO BE TETHERED

The court had delivered its sentence. But the real war was just beginning.

The civil case loomed—where restitution, damages, and the long shadow of betrayal would be measured not in years, but in dollars, documents, and dignity.

Justice, David quickly learned, wasn't measured in time. It was measured in recovery. And recovery, he realized, sometimes meant surrendering what could be reclaimed to protect what could still be rebuilt.

The authorities returned the duffel bag—roughly $200,000 in cash and checks. It was the only portion of his assets untouched by laundering. The rest—nearly $400,000—had vanished.

Between transfer fees, service charges, and the hidden costs of moving money through complex channels, he likely ended up with close to $300,000. The rest was swallowed by the expense of concealment.

Cassandra had played the role of seductress—emotional, visible, reckless. But Juan had played the long game.

He designed the con to vanish on contact. The offshore accounts, shell corporations, and falsified wire transfers weren't just tools—they were escape routes. By the time investigators traced one account, the funds had already split into five more. Nothing was recovered. Not a cent.

Juan exploited legal blind spots: Countries with strict privacy laws. Banks that ignored subpoenas. Shell entities engineered to dissolve on contact.

Without extradition treaties or financial disclosure agreements, recovery became a game of shadows. He hadn't just stolen money—he buried it in places the law couldn't reach.

While Cassandra faced cameras and courtrooms, Juan stayed quiet—calculating. He gave the DA just enough truth to sink her. Just enough cooperation to save himself.

He didn't just escape with leniency. He escaped with leverage.

Cassandra had nothing to show for two years of manipulation. What she believed would secure a lucrative future left her worse off than when she first met David.

David didn't call it justice. He called it air.

The court had ordered restitution. Cassandra and Juan were legally bound to repay every cent of the missing $400,000. On paper, it was justice. In practice, it was a tether.

David reviewed the payment schedules, the enforcement clauses, the projected timelines. Monthly installments. Wage garnishments. Supervised release.

Years of paperwork and reminders. Years of seeing their names on statements, hearing updates from clerks, waiting for checks that would never restore what was taken.

He met with Lillian one final time. She laid out his options: pursue enforcement, monitor compliance, reopen proceedings if they defaulted. Or—he could waive it. Not legally erase the debt but choose not to chase it.

David chose peace.

He signed the waiver in quiet ceremony. No press. No announcement. Just a pen, a witness, and a line that severed the last thread.

"I don't want their money," he said. "I don't want their names in my mailbox. I don't want to be paid back in pieces by people who never understood what they broke."

Lillian nodded. "Then we close the file."

And they did.

David left the courthouse with nothing new in his pocket—but something lighter in his chest. He hadn't recovered everything. But he had reclaimed himself.

After Cassandra's conviction, David's legal team moved swiftly. Lillian Cortez, his lead attorney, didn't file for divorce—she filed for annulment.

Her argument was clear: the marriage had never been valid in spirit or intent. It had been constructed on fraud.

Cassandra's motives, she contended, were exploitative from inception. The evidence was overwhelming: psychological evaluations, timelines of deceit, and documented manipulation.

Juan's testimony sealed it. Under oath, he stated that Cassandra's marriage to David was part of the con. She had planned it from the beginning—marry him, gain his trust, access his assets, and siphon funds once the emotional infrastructure was secure.

Juan described her strategy as calculated and rehearsed. She didn't fall in love. She built a blueprint.

Lester Vaughn, representing Cassandra, pushed back. He clung to marital statute, arguing that David had willingly given Cassandra access to his accounts, authorized her withdrawals, and treated her as a financial partner.

Vaughn insisted that Cassandra had contributed to the household and was entitled to joint property—even while incarcerated.

"She didn't steal," Vaughn said. "She was given access. She acted within the bounds of trust."

But Lillian cut through the argument with surgical precision.

"She wasn't a partner," she said. "She was a fraud. And fraud nullifies entitlement."

After three grueling months, the annulment was granted. The court ruled that the marriage was void because of the fraudulent intent.

Cassandra's legal status shifted—from estranged spouse to convicted fraudster with no marital claim.

But the battle wasn't over.

With the annulment in place, David's team launched a civil suit— brief, surgical.

Lillian argued not only for the restoration of David's assets, but for the complete invalidation of Cassandra's financial claims.

She laid out the fraud, the deception, the exploitation of trust.

Vaughn postured, citing shared expenses and household contributions, but the case was already sinking.

The judge ruled decisively.

Cassandra was not entitled to spousal assets. Her role had not been that of a partner, but of a predator.

The court found that her contributions were not genuine acts of partnership, but strategic moves in a long con.

David kept full ownership of the house, the retirement accounts, and all documented holdings. Cassandra's name was removed from all deeds, titles, and financial instruments.

The ruling was more than financial. It was a dismantling of illusion. Vaughn's defense collapsed under the weight of Cassandra's intent.

And in that moment, David felt the tether break. Cassandra, Juan, the con—finally behind him

CHAPTER 33

CHOOSING DIGNITY

David Ortiz—once unraveled, once deceived—didn't rebuild what he lost. He walked forward. He made something new.

The legal motions had ended. But the rebuilding hadn't.

It had been four and a half years since that September afternoon in 1989—since the day he met Cassandra and the slow unraveling began. Eight months of courtship that felt like rescue. Sixteen months of marriage that felt like certainty. And then almost three years of investigations, subpoenas, hearings, and litigation that felt like a second kind of grief.

What began as intimacy had become evidence. What once felt like partnership had been reduced to timelines and exhibits. Every month, every filing, every deposition chipped away at something he didn't know could break twice.

It had been nearly three years since Cassandra's arrest, two since her conviction—and still the erosion continued. The financial loss was staggering, siphoned through charm and precision. But it was the emotional breach that lingered. Cassandra hadn't just taken money. She'd taken trust, intimacy, and the quiet belief that love could be simple.

That spring, David planted a tree in the backyard—a Japanese maple, small and stubborn. He didn't name it. Didn't speak to it. He simply watered it, week after week.

It grew slowly. Like trust.

One morning, Reina asked why he'd chosen that spot. David looked out the window and answered without hesitation.

"It used to be where Elena liked to sit," he said. "Now it's mine."

The roots took hold. The leaves turned red.

And for the first time, David didn't think about what had been taken. He thought about what might still grow.

He didn't know what the next season would bring. But the soil was his. And this time, he'd choose what stayed.

The house that once held a promising future with Elena—and later, the illusion with Cassandra—had become unbearable. Every room echoed with contradiction. The garden Elena once tended had become a backdrop for Cassandra's performance. The walls remembered too much. The kitchen where she'd cooked, the bedroom where she'd lied—it was all part of the act.

After witnessing the betrayal in his own bedroom, David could no longer sleep there. The space felt contaminated—theatrical, false. He avoided it for weeks, sleeping on the couch, then in the guest room. Eventually, he gutted it: new paint, new floors, new furniture. He had to clear out the space before he could call it his again. Only then did he begin to sleep there—not as a return, but as a reclamation.

He tried to reclaim the house—repaint it, reimagine it, make it his again. But the silence remembered. The atmosphere hung heavy, dim and unyielding, as if betrayal had soaked into the walls. He told himself it was practical. But the truth was simpler: he couldn't live inside a memory that had been weaponized. The house itself had become a symbol of manipulation and loss—no longer a refuge, but a reminder.

Eventually, he decided to sell.

The house sold quietly. No open house. No bidding war. No farewell gathering. David had insisted on discretion. The buyers—a retired couple from Pennsylvania—fell in love with the antique garage and the view from the back deck. They knew nothing of its history. To them, it was a peaceful upstate New York gem. To David, it was a chapter he needed to close.

The night before the closing, he walked the hallway once more, pausing in each room to remember Elena. That night, he spoke to her spirit—voicing, for the first time, what had long remained unsaid.

I'm sorry, Elena. I brought her into the house we built together. She didn't deserve your walls, your garden, your echo. But I never stopped hearing you—even beneath her voice. You were my compass. Even when I lost the map—when I couldn't tell betrayal from love, or truth from illusion—you were still there, pointing me back to myself.

He hadn't come seeking forgiveness. He only needed to speak. And in speaking, something shifted—not erased but released. He needed to say it aloud—not for closure, but to name the betrayal, to honor the memory, and to begin, finally, moving forward.

He had loved Elena like gold—solid, luminous, enduring. She shaped the contours of his life without trying to own them. Even in silence, she was a presence. Even in absence, a guide.

Glass shimmered differently—sharp, seductive, and ultimately hollow. It reflected what he wanted to see until the illusion cracked. And when it shattered, it cut deep. He no longer mistook shine for substance. No longer confused proximity with intimacy. No longer believed performance could pass for truth. He didn't know if he'd love again. But if he did, it wouldn't be for rescue. It would be for resonance.

The fiscal damage had been resolved. But healing wasn't transactional. Grief charted its own course. And trust—trust had become a language he no longer spoke fluently. It wasn't just broken; it had been reprogrammed. He flinched at sincerity, second-guessed kindness, mistook warmth for strategy. Betrayal had rewired something.

What stung more than the money was how easily love had been monetized—and how long it took him to realize that trust isn't always reciprocal.

What endured was quieter: friendships that didn't flinch, family who held his name with care, memories that asked only to be remembered—not revised. And peace—not as recovery, but as something rarer: the grace of forward motion.

Some debts remain unsettled. Some scars refuse to fade completely. But sometimes, the story doesn't conclude with triumph.

It concludes in motion.

And sometimes, that motion is enough.

Sometimes a story doesn't end in triumph. It ends in movement. And sometimes, that's enough.

David needed time. Time to find himself, to understand who he was after the collapse, to discover where he could go without carrying the rubble of what he'd lived through. At forty two, he wasn't retired, but he felt worn from the inside out, as if he had aged in silence.

He requested a two month leave. His employer, aware of everything he had endured, agreed without conditions: no salary, no promises—just space. It was exactly what David needed: space to breathe, to think, to feel without obligation. He was exhausted... tired of meetings, deadlines. So he booked a one-way flight to Lisbon.

Elena had once danced with him in a narrow alley there, music spilling from a nearby café, her laughter echoing off the tiled walls. She called it "a city that remembers without asking."

From Portugal, he would go to Granada, then to the lavender fields of Provence, then to Kyoto in spring—each place chosen not for novelty, but for memory. They had dreamed of these places together. Now he would walk them alone, with her spirit as his companion.

But memory wasn't his only compass. David had always loved thoroughbreds—their elegance, their velocity, the way they carried history in muscle and motion. So wherever he traveled, he found the racetrack.

In Lisbon, he watched the morning gallop from the rail, mist rising off the turf. In Provence, he stood quietly at a country meet, the crowd sparse, the horses fierce. In Kyoto, he visited the paddock before the spring stakes, bowing slightly as the horses passed.

It wasn't about betting. It was about rhythm—about witnessing raw, unrestrained power push forward, relentless and unapologetic. That energy stirred something in him.

He craved movement—not just the physical pace of a gallop, but the distance it promised: from Cassandra, from the house, from the version of himself that once mistook glitter for grace.

He traveled light—just the essentials, a photograph of Elena tucked in his wallet, and a list of cities she once circled in a guidebook.

In Granada, he stood beneath the Alhambra's arches and whispered her name. In Provence, he danced alone in a field, letting the wind carry the rhythm. In Kyoto, beneath the cherry blossoms, David placed a smooth stone beneath a tree—a gesture for Elena. As he bowed his head, a different memory surfaced. Not of love, but of loss. The kind that wasn't poetic. The kind that was calculated.

Juan had pled guilty, testified, served his time, and walked free. According to Cassandra, he'd kept most of the money. David didn't know what to believe. But the outcome was clear: the money was gone.

The authorities called it sophisticated. David called it theft dressed as cooperation.

He didn't dwell on it. But he didn't forget it either.

He never retold the story. But once, in a coffee shop in Nova Scotia, a young barista asked why he always traveled alone. David stirred his mug and replied gently, "I don't travel alone. I travel with my silences." There was no follow-up. Only recognition.

In that time, David became something quieter than a legend—a man who had once lived beside ruin and chose, instead, to live beside rhythm. He walked coastal trails, lingered in pine forests, and traced maps that only mattered in fragments. He traveled not to escape, but to recalibrate.

After two months of travel, David returned to New York. Not to the man he was, but to the life he'd paused. He settled back in

New York—quietly, deliberately. Rejoined his family. Reentered his career. Not with triumph, but with steadiness. He was healed—not completely, but enough to reclaim what mattered. Enough to live without flinching. Enough to trust the rhythm he'd found.

He didn't go looking for love with urgency or fear. He'd learned to honor it—to recognize its weight and its fragility. He stayed open, but with a clarity he hadn't had before: intimacy couldn't be forced, and trust couldn't be improvised.

He didn't need a partner to feel whole, but he didn't close the door either. If life brought him something true, he would receive it without hurry. And if it never came, he was still at peace.

Some lives aren't defined by partnership. Some are defined by the dignity of choosing solitude over illusion. He had known love that was gold—solid, luminous, enduring.

And he had survived love that was glass—sharp, seductive, and ultimately hollow. He no longer confused the two. And that clarity, hard-won and quiet, was its own kind of grace.

He grew older. Forgot some names. But remembered patterns— the weight of trust, the sound of deception, the lightness of leaving.

Eventually, his belongings grew fewer: a box of journals, a photograph tucked quietly into a drawer—Elena's face half-lit, half-shadowed, as if memory itself had chosen the exposure.

Not everyone unravels loudly. Not everyone heals visibly. Some lives aren't reclaimed in sweeping arcs, but in quiet, steady loops—each silence shaped into new meaning.

And the road, as ever, didn't ask for permission. It simply continued.

And in the quiet between memory and motion, David chose dignity. Not as a destination—but as a way forward.

Healing isn't loud. But it is possible.

Even after betrayal. Even after silence.

Even after everything.

He didn't expect anything new to begin. Not at his age, not after everything. He had made peace with the idea that some lives are shaped not by partnership, but by clarity — by choosing solitude over illusion, truth over performance.

But life, as ever, had its own rhythm.

It happened on an ordinary Saturday in early autumn. David was at a small bookstore in the Village, the kind Elena used to love — narrow aisles, handwritten staff notes, a bell that chimed softly when the door opened. He wasn't looking for anything. He rarely was. He simply liked the quiet.

He reached for a book on the top shelf just as someone else reached for the same one. Their hands brushed — lightly, politely — and he stepped back.

"Please," he said. "Go ahead."

She smiled, warm but unassuming. Her hair was pulled back loosely, a few strands falling the way Elena's once did when she was reading on the couch. Not the same. Not even close. But something in the gentleness, the ease, the lack of performance — it stirred a memory without imitating it.

"I'm not in a rush," she said. "We can both look."

Her voice carried no urgency, no angle, no charm sharpened into strategy. Just presence. Simple, steady, human.

They spoke for a few minutes — about the author, about travel, about how some books find you when you're not looking. She laughed once, softly, and the sound didn't echo against old wounds. It landed somewhere new.

At the door, they paused at the same moment, each holding it open for the other. A small, shared smile.

"Would you...?" she began, then hesitated. "If you're not in a hurry, there's a café around the corner. I was going to sit and read for a bit."

David felt something shift inside him—quiet, steady, unmistakable.

"I'd like that," he said.

They walked out together, matching pace without trying, two strangers who suddenly didn't feel like strangers at all.

For the first time in years, the future didn't feel like something he had to survive. It felt like something he could meet.

BLANCA DE LA ROSA: BIOGRAPHY

Blanca De La Rosa, born in the Dominican Republic and raised in the projects of the upper west side of Manhattan, is the daughter of Dominican immigrants. Despite cultural and linguistic challenges, she graduated from Pace University with a degree in international business management. She built a successful 34-year career at Mobil Oil and later ExxonMobil Oil Corporation, rising through various domestic and international roles that took her across the U.S., Europe, Central/South America, and Nigeria.

As a business development manager and president of the company's Employee Resource Group, De La Rosa represented ExxonMobil at the Hispanic Heritage Foundation's Regional and National Scholarship Awards. She also served as a host, keynote speaker, and panelist at numerous events supported by the company's charity foundation. Her most rewarding role was mentoring younger employees through the corporate maze.

De La Rosa is a self-published author:

Self-help and career: "Empower Yourself for an Amazing Career" and "A Holistic Approach to Your Career," sharing career advice based on her successes. She combines practical, common-sense advice with inner wisdom and spirituality to provide strategies for workplace success.

Memoir/Autobiography: "Pursuing a Better Tomorrow" is an inspiring journey from Spain to the U.S., intertwining four stories that illustrate the challenges and opportunities of immigration, acculturation, coming of age, and self-discovery. De La Rosa shares her personal journey from New York City's projects to corporate

America, highlighting her growth and achievements despite numerous challenges.

Self-help and spiritual genre: "Your Power Within – Inner Guidance" It explores themes of personal growth, the soul's journey, inner strength, and the quest for purpose. The book emphasizes patience and gradual progress, guiding readers toward understanding and evolving through their experiences.

Fiction Novels: "The Betrayal: A Lifetime of Regrets" follows Camila, who discovers that sometimes we don't truly appreciate what we have until we lose it.

"Broken Vows: A Blessing in Disguise" tells the story of Mariana's awakening, as she realizes that at times what we're used to—the familiarity, the routine—binds us more than love itself. We stay because it's safe, because it's all we know... not because it's what we want.

BIBLIOGRAPHY

Memoir / Autobiography - *Stories of resilience, reinvention, and self-discovery*

 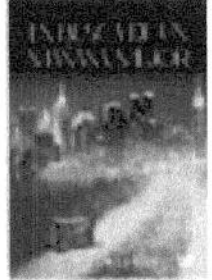

Pursuing a Better Tomorrow is a cross-generational story that spans more than a century, tracing the journey of one family who leaves behind the only world they know in search of hope and possibility. Through four interconnected narratives—from Spain to Cuba, the Dominican Republic, and New York—the novel explores immigration, acculturation, coming of age, and the courage required to build a new life. Blending historical context with personal stories, it illuminates the sacrifices, resilience, and cultural fusion that shape each generation's pursuit of a better future.

Children's Book

Leah's Skin Detective Story—gathering gentle clues about food, weather, feelings, and care that help her body feel calm again. As Leah explains what eczema feels like and what helps her, classmates learn how to listen, understand, and support. This warm, empowering story helps children with eczema feel seen and confident—and helps everyone else learn how to be kind, curious, and caring.

Fiction - *Love, betrayal, resilience — stories of the human heart*

From Gold to Glass is a haunting novel about love, grief, and the quiet vulnerabilities that make us human. Five years after losing his beloved wife Elena, David Ortiz opens his heart to Cassandra, a woman whose warmth and attentiveness mask a calculated design. What begins as solace becomes deception as Cassandra and her coconspirator study his habits, isolate his support system, and slowly dismantle the life he rebuilt. Moving between devotion and danger, memory and manipulation, the story explores how trust can be weaponized—and how a man learns to rise again when the love that shaped him becomes the love that undoes him.

The Betrayal / La Traición is a gripping portrait of a marriage undone by neglect, longing, and the quiet fractures that grow in the dark. Camila and Nic appear to have built a perfect life, but unmet needs and unspoken resentments push Camila toward an affair that shatters their family. Told through both perspectives, the novel traces the unraveling of their relationship—from the vibrant streets of New York City to the quiet suburbs of Virginia—as each confronts guilt, heartbreak, and the painful work of rebuilding. Exploring infidelity, family dynamics, and the ripple effects of broken trust, this story reveals the cost of betrayal and the difficult, redemptive path toward forgiveness and healing

Broken Vows / Votos Rotos - is a powerful story of love, betrayal, and the resilience required to rebuild a life shattered by deception. When Mariana Martinez discovers her husband Ricardo's affair, the world she built on loyalty and family collapses, forcing her to confront painful truths and uncover the strength she never knew she possessed. As Ricardo faces the consequences of his choices and Isabela grapples with the fallout of her own actions, each character is pushed toward reckoning and redemption. Through Mariana's journey of healing—anchored by her children and the unwavering support of her family—the novel explores the emotional cost of infidelity and the

Self-help / Spiritual - *Guides for inner strength, healing, and transformation*

Your Power Within — Inner Guidance - is a compassionate guide to rediscovering purpose, strength, and clarity after life's most profound losses. Blending personal reflection with spiritual insight, it explores the soul's journey, the quiet wisdom found in patience, and the inner power available to us in every season of life. Through themes of healing, self-discovery, and conscious evolution, the book invites readers to tap into their own inner guidance, break free from limiting beliefs, and embrace a life aligned with meaning, resilience, and joy.

Self-help / Career - *Wisdom for growth, leadership, and empowerment at work*

Unshaken is a bold manifesto and empowering guide that celebrates women's resilience, leadership, and unapologetic rise. Blending personal testimony, global insight, and cultural critique, it explores ambition, autonomy, visibility, and the quiet battles women fight every day. Structured in three parts—Rising Unapologetically, Toolkit for Resilience and Empowerment, and Living Unshaken—the book offers both inspiration and practical strategies for building confidence, navigating change, and leading with clarity and purpose. At its core, it honors the legacy of women who defy expectations and transform their strength into lasting impact.

A Holistic Approach to Your Career offers a practical, experience-driven guide to navigating the workplace with confidence, clarity, and resilience. Drawing on four decades of hard-earned corporate wisdom, it outlines the essential skills, habits, and mindsets needed to thrive— from managing difficult managers and recovering from career setbacks to building a strategic roadmap and assessing your professional journey with honesty. Blending personal stories with commonsense advice and inner guidance, the book provides a fresh, empowering approach for recent graduates, new employees, and anyone seeking direction, growth, and long-term success in their career.

Empower Yourself is a practical, holistic guide for anyone determined to reclaim their professional path. Drawing on decades of corporate experience, it blends personal stories with clear, actionable strategies to help readers assess where their career went off track, navigate difficult managers, recover from setbacks, and build a purposeful roadmap forward. With its mix of common sense wisdom and inner guidance, the book offers a fresh, empowering approach to rising with confidence and creating a career that is both successful and deeply fulfilling.